I LIVE IN YOUR BASEMENT!

I LIVE IN YOUR BASEMENT!

Look for more Goosebumps books
by R.L. Stine:
(see back of book for a complete listing)

Goosebumps®

I LIVE IN YOUR BASEMENT!

R.L. STINE

AN
APPLE
PAPERBACK

SCHOLASTIC INC.
New York Toronto London Auckland Sydney

A PARACHUTE PRESS BOOK

ISBN 0-590-39986-1

Copyright © 1997 by Parachute Press, Inc.
All rights reserved. Published by Scholastic Inc.
APPLE PAPERBACKS and logo are trademarks and/or registered trademarks of Scholastic Inc.
GOOSEBUMPS is a registered trademark of Parachute Press, Inc.

12 11 10 9 8 7 6 5 4 3 2 1   7 8 9/9 0 1 2/0

Printed in the U.S.A.   40

First Scholastic printing, November 1997

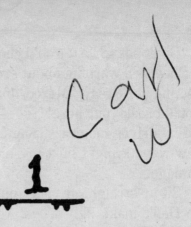

1

"'Don't do that. You'll poke your eye out.' That's what my mom says. No matter what I'm doing."

I told that to my friend Jeremy Goodman as we trotted to the playground behind our school.

Jeremy laughed. "Your mom really says that, Marco?"

I nodded and picked up the pace, keeping side by side with Jeremy as we crossed Fulton Street.

"Last night, I had a lot of homework," I told him. "I took out three new pencils and started to sharpen them. My mom came into the room and said, 'Don't do that. You'll poke your eye out.'"

Jeremy laughed again. "What does she want you to use? Crayons?"

I didn't laugh. It wasn't funny to me. I'm twelve years old, and my mom treats me like some kind of baby.

She's always warning me about *everything* I do.

"Don't climb that tree. You'll break your neck."

"Don't fill the bathtub so full. You'll drown."

"Don't eat so fast. You'll choke."

She has a warning about *everything!* I keep expecting her to say, "Marco, don't breathe so much. You'll break your nose!"

She drives me crazy. She constantly thinks up new ways I might hurt myself or do some kind of damage.

"Sit up straight or your spine will curve."

"Don't make ugly faces. Your face will freeze, and you'll always look like that."

"Don't pick your nose. Your finger will get stuck."

She's also the world's expert on germs. According to Mom, *everything* you touch or see will give you germs.

"Don't hug the dog. It has germs."

"Don't take a bite of Jeremy's candy bar. Germs."

"Don't put your hands in your pockets. Germs."

Mom is always on guard duty. Always alert. Always ready to step in and warn me about something.

It makes my life a little hard.

She doesn't like for me to play softball with my friends. She's sure I'll break my leg. That's if I'm lucky. If I'm unlucky, I'll break every bone in my body.

Do you know how *hard* it would be to break *every* bone in your body?

My mom is the only person in the world who thinks people do it every day of the week!

That's why I had to sneak out of the house to go play softball at the playground with Jeremy and some other kids from my school.

It was a warm, sunny day. The green lawns along Fulton Street all glowed in the sunlight. The air smelled fresh and sweet.

It felt so good to be jogging down the sidewalk with Jeremy, looking forward to playing a game, laughing and spending time with friends.

School had let out early because of some kind of teachers' meeting. I hurried home and dropped off my backpack.

The house was empty, except for Tyler, my dog. He's part cocker spaniel, part we-don't-know-what.

Tyler was happy to see me. He licked my face.

Mom doesn't like it when I let Tyler lick my face. You know why. The terrible "G" word.

Mom was out shopping or something. I guess she forgot that I'd be home early.

Such a lucky break. I changed into a ragged pair of jeans and a T-shirt. Then I grabbed my baseball glove and hurried out to meet Jeremy before Mom returned home.

"Marco, what would your mom do if she caught you playing softball?" Jeremy asked.

"Warn me," I replied. "She never punishes me or anything. She just warns me."

"My parents *never* warn me about anything," Jeremy said.

"That's because you're perfect!" I teased.

Jeremy slugged me on the arm.

Actually, I wasn't teasing. Jeremy *is* perfect. He gets all A's in school. He's good at sports. He takes care of his little sister. He almost never gets in trouble.

He doesn't touch anything with germs.

Perfect . . .

We passed the bus stop and crossed Fairchild Avenue. Our school came into view. It's a long, one-story building that stretches in a straight line for nearly a whole block.

The walls of the school are painted bright yellow. As yellow as an egg yolk. Mom says they discuss the color a lot at Parent Association meetings. No one likes it.

Jeremy and I jogged through the teachers' parking lot to the playground behind the building. The softball diamond stood behind the row of swings.

A bunch of kids were already there. I recognized Gwynnie Evans and Leo Murphy.

The Franklin twins were arguing as usual, standing nose to nose, screaming at each other. They're weird guys. You can never put them on the same team.

"You can start now!" Jeremy shouted. "The all-stars are here!"

He took off across the grass. Leo and some of the other kids called out to us.

I slowed to a walk, breathing hard. Jeremy is a lot better athlete than I am.

Gwynnie stood on the pitching mound, swinging two bats and talking to Lauren Blank. Gwynnie is always trying to prove that she's better in sports than any of the boys.

She's big and strong. She's at least half a foot taller than me, and she's got much bigger shoulders. She's always pushing kids around and acting tough.

No one likes her. But we always want her on our team because she can hit the ball a mile. And if some kind of argument breaks out, Gwynnie *always* wins it because she can yell the loudest.

"Let's get started," Jeremy declared.

"Who's choosing up sides?" I asked. "Who are the captains?"

Leo pointed. "Gwynnie and Lauren."

I took off running to the pitcher's mound. Gwynnie dropped one of the bats to the ground. She had the other one in her grip.

I guess she didn't see me.

As I ran up to her, she pulled the bat back — and swung it with all her might.

I saw the bat move.

But I didn't have time to duck or move out of the way.

5

The bat made a loud *THUNK* as it slammed into the side of my head.

At first, I didn't feel a thing.

The ground tilted up.

But I still didn't feel anything.

Then the pain exploded in my head.

Exploded . . . exploded . . . exploded.

Everything flashed bright red.

So bright, I had to shut my eyes.

I heard myself shrieking. Neighing like a horse. A shrill wail I never heard before.

And then the ground flew up to swallow me.

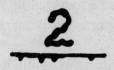

2

I woke up staring at the ceiling.

A blue ceiling light — blue as the sky — blurred then sharpened, blurred then sharpened above me.

Mom's face floated into view.

I blinked once. Twice. I knew I was home.

Mom's eyes were red and wet. She had her black hair pulled back tightly. But several strands had fallen loose and hung down her forehead.

Her chin trembled. "Marco —?"

I groaned.

My head ached. Everything ached.

I've done it, I thought. I've broken every bone in my body.

"Marco —?" Mom repeated in a whisper. "Are you waking up, dear?"

"Huh?" I groaned again.

Something was sitting on my head. Weighing me down.

Tyler? Why was the dog sitting on my head?

My arms ached as I slowly raised my hands to my head.

And felt a bandage. A heavy bandage.

I lowered my hands. The room began to spin. I gripped the couch cushions, holding on for dear life.

I stared up at the blue ceiling light until it came into focus. The den. I was lying on the soft leather couch in the den.

Mom floated into view again, her chin still trembling. She pulled a blanket up nearly to my chin. "Marco? You're awake?" she repeated. "How do you feel?"

"Great," I muttered.

Talking made my throat hurt.

She stared down at me. "Can you see me, dear? It's me. Your mom."

"Yeah. I can see," I whispered.

She wiped one eye with a tissue. Then she stared at me some more.

"I can see fine," I told her.

She patted my chest over the blanket. "That's good, dear."

I groaned in reply.

Please don't say, I told you so! I thought. I crossed my fingers, even though it hurt to cross them. And I prayed. *Please don't say I told you so.*

Mom's expression changed. She frowned at me. "I *told* you not to play baseball," she said.

"It wasn't baseball," I choked out. "It was softball."

"I *told* you not to play," Mom said sternly. "But you didn't listen to me. And now you've cracked your head open like an eggshell."

"Huh?" I gasped. "Cracked it open? Mom, will I be okay?"

She didn't answer.

"Will I?" I demanded. "Tell me the truth. What did the doctor say, Mom? Will I be okay?"

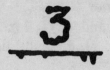

3

"Of course," she replied. Her face floated over me for a second, then slid out of view.

I didn't like the way she said it. It sounded false. Too cheerful.

"Tell me the truth," I insisted. "Am I really going to be okay?"

No answer.

I lifted my head. Sharp pain shot down the back of my neck.

Mom had vanished from the room. I could hear her putting plates away in the kitchen.

I tried calling her. But my voice came out in a hoarse whisper.

I lowered my head slowly to the couch cushion and shut my eyes.

I guess I drifted off to sleep. The ringing phone woke me up.

I blinked up at the blue ceiling light, forcing it to come into focus. The phone rang and rang. I waited for Mom to pick it up. But she didn't answer it.

Did she go out and leave me all alone? I wondered. She wouldn't do that. Where is she?

Groaning, I rolled onto my side and grabbed the phone off the coffee table. I raised it to my ear.

"Owww!"

I banged it too hard against the bandage over my head. The side of my head throbbed with pain.

"Hello?" I croaked.

I heard breathing on the other end. And then a voice I didn't recognize said, "I hope you're okay, Marco."

"Who — who is this?" I stammered. I shut my eyes tight, trying to push away the pain of my throbbing head.

"I hope you're okay," the voice repeated. A boy's voice. "I don't want anything bad to happen to you."

"Huh? You don't?" I murmured. "Uh . . . thanks." I kept my eyes shut. The pain pulsed at my temples. It was hard to hold the phone over the heavy bandage.

"Who *is* this?" I demanded again.

"I don't want anything bad to happen to you," the boy said again. "Because you're going to take care of me from now on."

"Excuse me?" I choked out. "I don't understand."

11

Silence at the other end.

I took a deep breath. I decided to ask the question one more time. "Who is this?"

"It's me," the voice replied. "Keith."

"Keith?"

"Yes. Keith."

"I — I don't know you," I stammered.

"You should," the boy replied softly. "You should know me, Marco. I live in your basement."

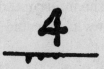

Did I hang up? Or did Keith hang up?

I'm not sure. I felt very confused, very upset.

Keith hadn't called to be friendly. I knew he was trying to scare me.

But, why?

Was it actually a friend of mine? Someone from school playing a joke? It wasn't a very funny joke.

I stared at the ceiling, feeling groggy and weak. I don't know how much time passed.

I kept picturing Gwynnie standing on the pitcher's mound. I saw her swinging two bats. Then one. I saw the bat whirling toward my head.

"Ohhh." I uttered a low moan and forced the picture from my mind.

"How are you doing, Marco?" a voice whispered.

I gazed up at Mom. She had brushed her hair and put on lipstick. She had changed into a bright green T-shirt and a dark skirt.

"Feeling better?" she asked. "I brought you a

13

bowl of cereal. You should try eating something. If you don't eat, acid will burn a hole in your stomach."

"Mom — the phone," I started groggily. "It rang and —"

"Yes, I know," she interrupted. "It was Jeremy. He wanted to know if he could come over to see you."

"Huh? Jeremy?"

She nodded. "I told him you weren't quite ready for visitors. I said he could probably come tomorrow."

"I didn't mean that call," I said. I pulled myself up onto my elbows. My head didn't throb as badly. The room didn't spin and tilt.

I was starting to feel a little stronger.

"I got another call," I told her. "You didn't pick up, so I answered it."

"But, Marco —" Mom started.

"It was from a strange boy," I continued. "It was a very weird call. He said his name was Keith. And he said he lived in our basement."

Mom's expression changed. She lowered her eyes. "Oh, wow," she murmured.

"It was kind of a frightening call," I said. "Why would somebody call and say they lived in our basement?"

Mom placed a cool hand on my hot forehead. "I — I'm a little worried about you, Marco," she said softly.

14

"Huh? What do you mean?"

"You have to take things slowly," she replied. "You didn't listen to my warnings. And you had a very bad hit on the head."

"But, Mom, that phone call I got —"

Her chin quivered again. "You're not thinking clearly, Marco," she said.

"Why? Why do you say that?" I demanded.

She narrowed her eyes at me. "There's no phone in this room," she said.

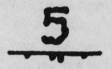

5

I woke up early the next morning. I sat up, feeling alert. Refreshed. Before I even stood up, I knew I was a lot better.

My head didn't throb. My muscles didn't ache.

I took a long shower. The water felt so crisp and sharp on my skin.

I was drying myself when I realized I no longer had the bandage on my head. I spotted it on the floor by my bed. I guessed it had fallen off during the night.

Stepping up to the medicine chest mirror, I checked out the damage. Not too bad. I had an ugly purple bruise on my right temple. It had swelled up like a giant mosquito bite.

But the rest of my head had its normal shape.

I winked at myself. My eyes seemed sharp and clear.

I let out a loud cheer. My throat didn't hurt. I was so happy to be feeling strong again.

I pulled on a pair of baggy jeans and a sweat-

shirt. And I hurried down to the kitchen for breakfast.

"Don't run in the kitchen like that," Mom warned. "You'll bang into the counter and break your kneecap."

Kneecap?

That was a *new* one!

"I'm starving!" I cried. I poured myself a big bowl of my favorite cereal combo — Frosted Flakes and Corn Pops, all mixed together. I grabbed a spoon and began gobbling hungrily.

"Don't eat cereal so fast," Mom warned. "It'll clog your stomach pipes."

I'd heard that one before.

"Guess you're feeling better," Mom said. She smiled at me and squeezed my hand.

I nodded. "I feel fine," I told her. "What day is it?"

"Saturday," she replied. Her smile faded. "I'm glad you're feeling better. But I want you to stay in today."

"You always want me to stay in," I grumbled.

"You're still weak," she said. "You might faint and hit your head on the sidewalk."

"I'll stay in," I promised.

A loud *THUD THUD* made me jump. "What was *that?*" I yelped.

Mom stood up. She studied me. "It's just someone knocking on the door," she said. "See? You're still not yourself, Marco."

"I *said* I won't go out," I groaned.

Jeremy came into the kitchen. He stopped halfway across the room and stared at me. "Are you alive?" he asked.

I pinched my arm. "Yeah," I told him.

"Don't pinch yourself. You'll make a bruise," Mom warned.

Jeremy didn't come any closer. He stood in the middle of the kitchen and stared at me.

"Why don't you sit down while I finish my cereal?" I asked him. "It's okay to come over here. You won't catch what I've got."

"Did you eat breakfast?" Mom asked Jeremy. "Never go out on an empty stomach. Your whole system will stop working."

Jeremy walked slowly to the table. "I just keep picturing Gwynnie swinging that bat," he said. He swallowed hard. "It was so horrible. I saw the whole thing."

He dropped into the chair next to me and sighed. "I thought she knocked your head off, Marco. I really did. I was sick. I thought I was going to heave up my lunch on the grass."

"Don't talk about heaving at the breakfast table," Mom scolded. She started for the door. "I have to leave for a short while, Marco. Remember your promise. Don't go out."

"I remember," I muttered.

"And take it easy," she instructed. "Just sit and talk. Don't do anything else. You'll pass out."

18

When she disappeared, Jeremy turned to me. "You really okay?" he asked.

I nodded. "Yeah. I don't feel bad at all." I finished the last of the cereal and poured myself a glass of orange juice. "I feel a lot better than yesterday," I declared.

"Gwynnie called me last night," Jeremy said. "She wanted to know how you were doing. She was really messed up. You know. About hitting you."

I snickered. "You mean she didn't brag about what a great swing she has?"

"No way!" Jeremy insisted.

"Well, it wasn't her fault," I said. "I ran right into her bat. It was a real smooth move."

We talked about the accident for a while longer. Then I asked Jeremy if he wanted to feel the purple bump on the side of my head.

"Hey — no way!" he cried, making a sick face.

I knew that would gross him out.

He helped me put away the breakfast stuff. "What do you want to do?" I asked him.

"Your mom said you can't go out," Jeremy reminded me.

"So we'll stay in," I replied.

"Want to play pool?" he suggested.

We have a pool table in our basement. It's a regulation-size table, and there isn't quite enough room for it. You have to tilt your pool cue up and play around the concrete beams.

19

"Yeah. I'll play you," I agreed. He's a much better pool player than I am. But sometimes I get lucky and beat him.

I finished shoving the breakfast dishes into the dishwasher. Then I led the way to the basement door.

I reached for the doorknob — then stopped.

I live in your basement.

I remembered the boy's voice on the phone. So flat and cold.

You're going to take care of me from now on. . . . I live in your basement.

His words came back to me. They made me hesitate at the door.

But I only imagined that call, I told myself.

There was no boy. No voice. No Keith.

I imagined it because I got hit on the head.

Right?

I pulled open the door. I gazed down the basement steps.

Then, gripping the banister, I led the way down.

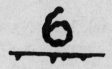

6

As soon as I reached the basement, I ran around turning on all the lights. Even in the laundry room.

Jeremy picked up a pool cue and began to chalk the tip. "What is your problem, Marco?" he called. "Are we going to play or not?"

"I like a lot of light," I told him.

I peeked behind the big stack of cartons near the furnace. Then I squeezed behind the furnace to see if anyone was living back there.

Nothing but a tall mountain of dust. I was beginning to feel a little silly.

Why would anyone be living in my basement? The whole idea was crazy.

I trotted over to the pool table and picked out a cue. Then Jeremy and I began to play.

He sank the three ball in a side pocket. On his next shot, balls clattered all over the table. But nothing dropped in.

My turn. I had to squeeze between the table and

a concrete pole and tilt the cue up toward the ceiling. Not an easy shot.

I missed everything.

"Did you ever play pool with Gwynnie?" Jeremy asked, moving around the table to find his best shot.

"No. Never," I told him. "Is she any good?"

He snickered. "She plays pool the way she plays softball. She hits the balls so hard, she *cracks* them. A bunch of us were playing once at the Youth Center. Gwynnie sent a ball flying off the table, and it sailed out the window!"

"Maybe she thinks she has to hit a home run!" I joked.

We both laughed. Laughing made the side of my head hurt.

Thinking about Gwynnie made my head hurt!

Jeremy bounced the seven ball into the eight ball. The eight ball almost dropped into a corner pocket. "That was close!" He sighed.

Maybe you don't know the rules of pool. If the eight ball goes in, you lose.

That's the only way I ever beat Jeremy.

"The Franklin twins were playing at the Youth Center too," Jeremy continued. "And they got into a fight."

I rolled my eyes. "So what else is new?"

"It was so dumb," Jeremy said. "They were arguing over which is the six ball and which is the nine ball. They started fencing with their pool cues. And then they smeared blue chalk all over each other."

"Nice," I murmured. I hit the twelve ball a solid shot, but it didn't go in. "Why do you think the Franklin twins fight all the time?" I asked.

Jeremy thought about it for a moment. "Because they're twins," he said finally. "Even *they* can't tell each other apart. And so they have to prove they're different from each other."

"That's very deep," I replied. I wanted to think about that.

But a strange sound made me spin away from the table.

A scratching sound. Very close.

A scratch. Then a *BUMP*.

"Did you hear that?" I whispered to Jeremy.

He nodded. "Yes." He pointed to the stairs.

Another *BUMP*.

We have a large pantry cabinet under the stairwell. The noises were coming from inside the cabinet.

We both stared at the wooden cabinet door.

Another *BUMP*.

"There's someone in there," I muttered. "Someone trying to get out."

Jeremy narrowed his eyes at me. "Why would someone be hiding in your cabinet?"

I made my way over to the cabinet door. "Who's in there?" I called.

No reply.

A scraping sound. Someone right behind the door.

"Who is it?" I repeated.

No reply.

I grabbed the cabinet door. Took a deep breath. Tugged it open.

And screamed as a creature leaped out at me.

7

"A squirrel!" Jeremy cried.

Yes. A fat gray squirrel jumped from the closet — onto my leg.

It fell off. Hit the floor, its eyes wild, its legs thrashing the air. Sliding on the linoleum, it took off across the basement.

"How did a squirrel get in there?" Jeremy asked.

I was still too startled to reply. I watched the squirrel try to climb one of the concrete beams. It slipped off, turned, and ran toward the laundry room.

I finally found my voice. "We've got to get it out of here!" I shrieked. "Mom freaks out when animals get in the house. You know. They have germs."

The squirrel was staring back at us from the laundry room door. "Get him!" I cried.

Jeremy and I chased after the squirrel.

It darted around the laundry room. Behind the dryer. Nowhere to run now.

"I've got it!" I shrieked. I stretched out my hands and made a wild dive.

But the squirrel scampered right over my back. Dodged past Jeremy. And raced back into the main room.

My head started to throb. I was breathing hard.

I darted out of the laundry room. The squirrel ran under the pool table, its bushy tail standing straight up.

I checked to make sure both basement windows were open. Then I grabbed an old fishing net from against the wall.

The frightened animal stopped running and turned back to Jeremy and me. Its whole body trembled. Its little black eyes pleaded with us.

"Here, squirrel! Here, squirrel!" I called to it, waving the net. "We're not going to hurt you."

I swiped the net at it. Missed.

The squirrel took off. Jeremy dove for it. He missed too.

As we watched helplessly, the squirrel jumped onto the pile of cartons by the furnace. Climbed to the top. And leaped out of the basement window.

"Yesssss!" Jeremy and I both cheered and slapped each other a high five.

"Victory over all squirrels!" Jeremy boomed in his deepest voice.

I didn't know what that was supposed to mean. But we both burst out laughing.

Mom's voice from the top of the stairs cut our laughter short. "What's going on down there?" she called.

"Nothing," I replied quickly. "Just playing pool."

"Marco — be careful with those pool sticks," she shouted. "You'll poke your eye out."

Jeremy and I played a few games. He beat me easily each time. But we had fun. And we didn't poke out any eyes.

Mom made us sandwiches and chicken noodle soup for lunch. She kept warning us to blow on the soup or else we'd burn the skin off our tongues.

Yuck.

After lunch, I started to feel tired. So Jeremy went home.

"Go up to your room and watch TV or take a nap," Mom advised. "I warned you not to overdo it."

"I didn't overdo it," I grumbled. But I went upstairs and took a long nap.

Too long. Late that night, I couldn't get to sleep. I felt wide awake.

I read for a while. Then I did a little channel surfing, but I didn't find anything good to watch.

I glanced at my bed table clock. A few minutes after midnight.

My stomach growled. Maybe I need a midnight snack, I decided.

I clicked on the hall light and made my way downstairs to the kitchen. But I didn't get as far as the kitchen. To my surprise, the basement door stood open.

"Weird," I muttered. Mom always keeps that door closed. She's a nut about keeping doors shut.

I walked over to the door. And started to push it closed.

But I stopped when I heard a scraping sound down there.

Footsteps?

I poked my head into the opening and peered down into the darkness. "Who — who's down there?" I called.

I heard more scraping steps.

And then a boy's voice called up. "It's me. Keith. Don't you remember? I live down here."

8

"No! You don't exist!"

The words burst from my mouth. My cry sounded shrill and frightened.

I heard more footsteps on the linoleum floor. Then the basement light flashed on.

And I stared down at — Mom!

"Huh?" I gasped.

"Marco — why aren't you asleep?" she demanded, frowning up at me, hands at her waist.

"Uh . . . because I'm awake," I replied. "Mom, what are you doing down there?"

"Laundry," she said. "I couldn't sleep, either. So I decided to do laundry. You know. It always relaxes me."

"Mom — come upstairs. Now!" I cried. "There's someone down there with you!"

She squinted up at me. Tilted her head, examining me with her eyes. "What do you mean?" she asked softly.

"Hurry!" I insisted. "That boy. He talked to me

again. He's down there, Mom. He says he *lives* down there."

"Marco, I'm worried about you," Mom said calmly. She started up the stairs, her eyes locked on me. "You're not making any sense, dear."

"But I *am!*" I insisted. "I heard him, Mom. He talked to me — just now! He's down there! Really!"

"It's too late to call Dr. Bailey," she fretted. She stepped up beside me and pressed her palm against my forehead. "No fever."

"Mom — I'm not imagining it!" I wailed.

"Tomorrow is Sunday," she said. "I want you to rest all day. Then we'll see if you are ready to go back to school on Monday."

"But, Mom —" I started. "I —"

The boy's voice interrupted me from downstairs. "Marco," he called, "listen to your mother."

"Mom — did you *hear* that?" I shrieked.

"Hear what?" Mom demanded, eyeing me sharply.

"The boy —" I started. But I didn't finish. Someone bumped me hard from behind.

I stumbled toward the basement — and nearly fell down the stairs.

"Whoa —!" I let out a cry and spun around.

Tyler wagged his tail at me. He shuffled forward and bumped me again. He does that all the time. Just to be friendly, I guess.

"You stupid dog!" I shrieked. "You nearly *killed* me!"

Tyler stopped wagging. He stared up at me with his big brown eyes.

"Don't yell at the dog," Mom scolded. "You're really not doing well, Marco. Let's tuck you in, okay? You are definitely overtired."

"But, Mom —"

I decided not to argue. What was the point?

I glanced down into the basement, hoping to

catch a glimpse of the boy. But I saw only darkness.

Where was he? Where was he hiding?

I knew I hadn't imagined him. I knew I had really heard him.

So what was going on?

Mom let me go to school on Monday. The way things turned out, I wished she had kept me home.

I felt fine. The bump on my head was still purple. But it had shrunk to about the size of a quarter.

When I went into the school building, everyone ran up to me. The Franklin twins were arguing about which backpack was whose. They are always getting their stuff mixed up.

But when they saw me, they dropped both backpacks and hurried over.

"Marco — how are you?"

"Are you okay?"

"Let me see your bruise."

"Wow. That's real ugly!"

"Does it hurt?"

"I can't believe you're back!"

"You must have a really hard head!"

Everyone laughed and joked and made a big fuss over me. I enjoyed being the center of attention for once. Usually, no one pays any attention to me at all!

I was feeling pretty good about things.

Until the bell rang and Miss Mosely asked me to come up to the front of the class. "I think we're all glad to see you in school today, Marco," she said.

Jeremy started clapping, and then everyone else clapped. Even Gwynnie, who sits right in front of the teacher.

"Since we've been studying health care," Miss Mosely continued, "I want you to tell everyone what it was like in the hospital."

Hospital?

I stared at her. My brain did a flip-flop. My mouth dropped open.

Had I been in the hospital?

"What was your room like in the hospital?" Miss Mosely asked. "What kind of doctor examined you? What did the doctor look for?"

I blinked. Thinking hard. Trying to remember.

"Tell us everything," Miss Mosely insisted. She crossed her arms and stared at me through her round, black-framed eyeglasses, waiting for me to talk.

"I — I don't remember," I stammered.

One of the Franklin twins laughed. A few kids whispered to each other.

"Well, what *do* you remember about the hospital, Marco?" Miss Mosely asked, speaking slowly and clearly as if talking to a three-year-old.

"I don't remember anything. Nothing at all!" I blurted out.

Gwynnie leaned forward so that she practically hung over Miss Mosely's desk. "Maybe I should hit him on the head again," she said. "You know. To help bring back his memory."

A few kids laughed.

Miss Mosely frowned at Gwynnie. "That's a *terrible* thing to say. It's not a joke. Memory loss from a hit on the head can be very serious."

Gwynnie shrugged her big shoulders. "Just kidding," she muttered. "Can't anyone take a joke?"

Meanwhile, I was still standing up there in front of everyone. Feeling awkward and confused.

Why didn't I remember the hospital? The first thing I remembered, I was lying on the den couch at home.

Miss Mosely motioned for me to sit down. "We're glad you're okay, Marco," she said. "And don't worry about the things you forgot. Your memory will come back."

Up till then, I didn't know it had *left*. I dropped into my seat, feeling weak and shaken.

The rest of the day was a blur.

I was still thinking hard that afternoon as I started walking home. Still trying to remember *something* about the hospital.

I saw some kids starting a softball game on the playground diamond. Thinking about softball gave me a chill.

I started to turn away — but someone caught my eye.

Gwynnie!

She came chasing after me across the grass. She carried a baseball bat, raised high over her head.

She had a grim, determined look on her face.

"Marco! Hey — Marco!" she called, waving the bat menacingly.

She's going to hit me again, I knew.

But, *why?*

"No —!" I let out a cry. And gaped at her in horror.

"Gwynnie — please don't!"

10

"Marco! Hey — Marco!"

Gwynnie had a fierce look on her face. She swung the bat over her head again.

I froze. My legs refused to move.

With a loud cry, I finally managed to turn away. And I started to run.

I hurtled across the street without checking for traffic. What is her problem? Is she *crazy*? I asked myself. Why is she doing this?

Did Gwynnie really think she could bring back my memory with a smack on the head?

I turned the corner, breathing hard, the backpack bouncing on my shoulders. Glancing back, I saw her on the other side of the street. Two school buses rumbled by, forcing her to wait.

I lowered my head, shifted the backpack, and forced myself to pick up speed.

By the time I reached home, my heart pounded so hard it hurt. And the bump on my head throbbed with pain.

I dove into the house and slammed the door behind me. Then I pressed my back against the door and struggled to catch my breath.

"Marco? Is that you?" Mom called from the den.

Still gasping for breath, I tried to choke out an answer. But only a low croaking sound escaped my throat.

Mom appeared in the living room doorway. She narrowed her eyes, studying me. "How was your first day back?"

"Okay," I managed to murmur.

"You didn't overdo it — did you?" she demanded. "Why do you look so pale? Did you take gym, Marco? I gave you a note to excuse you from gym — remember?"

"We . . . didn't . . . have . . . gym," I gasped.

Mom was always giving me notes to excuse me from gym. She was sure I'd poke my eye out or break every bone in my body in gym class.

"Why are you so out of breath?" she asked, crossing the room to me. She placed a hand on my forehead. "You're sweating. Didn't I warn you about sweating? It'll give you a cold."

"Really. I'm fine," I said, starting to feel normal again. I slipped out from under her hand and peeked out the front window.

Had Gwynnie chased me all the way home?

I didn't see her out there.

"I felt okay today," I told her. "No problem."

I wanted to ask her about the hospital. But I

37

didn't want her to know that I'd lost my memory. It would only cause a lot more trouble.

So I didn't say anything about it. Instead, I made my way to the stairs. "I've got a lot of homework to catch up on," I told her. "I'll be up in my room."

"Do you want a snack?" she called after me. "You shouldn't do homework on an empty stomach."

"No thanks," I replied. I climbed the stairs and hurried down the hall.

I stopped in the doorway.

And let out a startled cry when I saw a boy sitting on my bed.

He looked about my age. He had wavy black hair around a thin, serious face. He gazed at me with round dark eyes. Sad eyes. He wore black denim jeans and a loose-fitting plaid flannel shirt.

He didn't appear at all surprised to see me.

"Who — who are you?" I stammered.

"It's me. Keith," he replied softly. "I told you. I live in your basement."

11

I didn't say anything. My mind went blank. I stared at the boy from out in the hall.

My knees suddenly felt weak and trembly. I grabbed the sides of the doorframe to keep from falling.

A cruel smile spread slowly over Keith's face. His dark eyes flashed. "Come in. I thought we should get to know each other," he said. "Since you are going to take care of me from now on."

I swallowed hard.

I stood there frozen for a long moment.

And then I screamed, "No! No way!"

I pulled the bedroom door shut. It had a key and a lock, which we never use.

My hand trembled as I grabbed the key and turned it.

I tested the door.

Yes! I had locked Keith in. He was trapped inside my bedroom.

Now Mom would see him. Now she would *have* to believe me.

"Mom!" I shouted. "Come up here! Hurry!"

No reply.

Had she gone out?

No. She was probably in the kitchen starting dinner.

I tested the door again, making sure it was locked tight. Then I plunged down the stairs, calling to her.

"Marco? What on earth —?" She came running from the kitchen, carrying an onion and a knife.

"Come upstairs! Hurry!" I cried. "I've caught him! He's in my room!"

"Caught who?" She eyed me suspiciously. "Who is in your room?"

"The boy!" I shouted. I grabbed her by the arm and started to pull her up the stairs. "Keith. The boy who lives in the basement."

"Marco — wait." Mom tugged her arm free. "Please don't start that again. You know how worried I get when you start talking crazy."

"I'm not crazy!" I wailed.

I grabbed her arm again. The onion fell out of her hand and bounced across the floor.

"Stop pulling me. I'm coming," she snapped. "You're acting very strange, Marco. I don't like this one bit. Dr. Bailey said that if you started acting in a weird manner, I should call him immediately and —"

40

"Mom — just don't talk!" I begged. "Don't say another word. Please — follow me. He's in my room. I locked him in. You'll see him with your own eyes. Then you'll know I'm not crazy."

She grumbled, but she followed me up the stairs.

I stopped outside my room and reached for the key. My heart pounded so hard, I thought my chest might explode. My head started to throb.

I turned the key. And pushed open my bedroom door.

"There!" I declared, pointing to my bed.

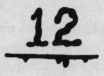

12

Mom and I both let out cries of surprise.

Tyler sat staring at us from the bed.

He panted loudly. His tongue hung out. When he saw us, his tail started to wag.

Mom placed a firm hand on my shoulder. "Go lie down on that bed, Marco," she ordered. "I'm calling the doctor right now."

"No. Wait," I insisted. I ducked out from under her grip.

I dropped to the floor and peered under the bed. "Keith — where are you?"

Not under there.

I climbed to my feet, ran across the room, and tugged open the closet door. "Keith —?"

No.

I spun around. Where else could he be hiding?

Tyler leaped off the bed and bounded from the room.

"That poor dog doesn't like being locked up," Mom fretted.

"I didn't lock him in here!" I shouted. "I locked Keith in."

She *tsk-tsked*. "You're going to be fine, Marco. Really you are." Her voice trembled.

It was easy to figure out what she really meant: *That hit on the head scrambled your brains, Marco. You're acting like a total nutcase!*

I took a deep breath and tried to explain again. "Mom, I don't know how Tyler got in here. But I do know there was a boy in my room. And I locked him in."

"I'm going to phone Dr. Bailey right now," Mom replied. "But I don't want you to worry. Everything will be okay." She hurried from the room.

Everything will be okay. Mom's words lingered in my mind.

As usual, she was wrong.

Dr. Bailey's waiting room was all blue and green. A huge fish tank against one wall bubbled quietly. The blue and green chairs, blue and green carpet, and blue and green walls made me feel as if I were in a fish tank too!

Mom and I checked in with the woman behind the desk. Then we sat down on a hard plastic couch against the wall.

On the plastic chairs across from us, a girl sat with her father. The girl was about seven or eight. Every few seconds, she hiccupped loudly. Her whole body shook with each hiccup.

"She's been doing that for two weeks," her father explained, shaking his head.

"Dad," the girl snapped, "it's only been *HIC* ten days."

"Has she been eating eggs?" Mom asked the father. "Too many eggs can give you the hiccups."

The man stared at Mom.

"It's the egg whites," Mom continued. "They're too slippery. You can't digest them."

The man stared at Mom some more. Finally he murmured, "I don't think it was eggs."

The girl hiccupped and shook.

The fish tank bubbled.

I felt as if I were swimming with the fish. Floating through thick blue water.

But I can't breathe underwater! I told myself.

The girl hiccupped again.

The sound was starting to drive me crazy. I wanted to go home. I turned to Mom, who had picked up a magazine and was thumbing through it. "Can we go?" I pleaded. "I'm okay."

She shook her head. "Dr. Bailey just wants to look at you," she replied, keeping her eyes on the magazine. "A hit on the head is serious. You only have one head, you know."

The girl hiccupped.

"Try holding your breath," her father instructed her.

"I've been holding it for ten days!" she grumbled.

Several hundred hiccups later, the nurse led

44

Mom and me into Dr. Bailey's office. As I stepped inside, I saw that his office was blue and green too.

The doctor was a cheerful, chubby man. He had a round face, a shiny, bald head, and he wore a bow tie under his green lab coat. The bow tie bobbed up and down on his Adam's apple when he talked.

He came around the desk to shake hands with me. Then he used his thumbs to pull up my eyelids so that he could examine my eyes.

"Hmmm . . . looks okay," he murmured.

He ran his thumb gently over the bump on my head. "Does that hurt, Marco?"

"A little," I confessed.

"It's healing nicely," he told Mom. "Very nicely indeed. Now what seems to be the problem, Marco?"

I hesitated. Should I tell him about Keith? If I do, will he think I'm crazy too? Will he send me back to the hospital or something?

Should I tell him I don't remember anything about being in the hospital?

Dr. Bailey gazed at me patiently, waiting for me to begin.

Finally, I decided, okay, I'll tell him everything. He's a doctor, after all. He will understand.

So I told him I couldn't remember the hospital. And then I told him about the boy who said he lived in our basement. And I told him about actually seeing Keith. And locking him in my room. And finding Tyler.

The whole story. I told him everything. It felt good to tell it.

Dr. Bailey sat behind his desk and kept his eyes locked on me the whole time. His bow tie twitched on his Adam's apple. But he didn't say a word until I finished.

Then he leaned forward and sighed. "It doesn't sound too bad," he said.

"Oh, thank goodness!" Mom exclaimed.

Dr. Bailey scratched his bald head. "But do you know what I would like to do just to make sure everything is okay?" he asked.

"What?" Mom and I said together.

"I'd like to remove your brain and examine it under a microscope," Dr. Bailey said.

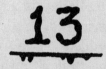

13

"Huh?" I gasped. I nearly fell out of my chair.

"It isn't a difficult operation," Dr. Bailey said, flashing me a calm, reassuring smile.

"But — but —" I sputtered.

"Once I crack the skull open, the brain slides out easily," the doctor explained.

"I — I don't think so," I protested.

He shrugged. His bow tie hopped up and down on his throat. "I can't really see the brain clearly unless I remove it."

My heart was pounding. My hands were suddenly icy cold. I studied Dr. Bailey's round face. "You're joking — right?" I demanded. "This is some kind of a sick joke?"

Mom nudged me in the side. "Listen to the doctor," she said. "The doctor knows what he's talking about. If he says the brain comes out, it comes out."

Dr. Bailey leaned farther across the desk. His face loomed so close, I could see tiny beads of sweat on his forehead. "It won't hurt much," he said.

I turned to Mom. "You're not going to let him do it — are you?" I demanded.

She patted my hand. "Whatever the doctor thinks is best. Dr. Bailey is a very good doctor, Marco. Very experienced."

The doctor nodded. "I've removed a lot of brains," he told me. "I don't mean to brag, but —"

"Can Mom and I talk about this?" I asked, stalling for time. "Can we come back tomorrow or something? I feel fine. Really, I do. In fact, I feel *excellent!*"

Dr. Bailey scratched his bald head again. "That's a good idea," he replied to my mom. "Why don't you call me tomorrow? We can schedule the de-braining then."

The *what*?

The *de-braining*?

I jumped up from my chair and darted for the door. I didn't wait for Mom. I didn't say good-bye. I just ran.

Mom followed me into the waiting room. "Marco, that was really rude of you!" she scolded.

"I'd like to keep my brain," I replied angrily, and kept walking to the office door. As we passed, I said good-bye to the girl with hiccups.

"Hic Hic Hic," she said. I think her problem was getting worse!

"Doctors know what's best," Mom said, hurrying across the parking lot after me.

I climbed into the car and crossed my arms over my chest. "I'm perfectly okay, Mom," I told her through gritted teeth. "My brain is totally normal. I'll never see that boy Keith again. He's gone forever. I know he is. I'll never see or hear him again."

But of course I was wrong.

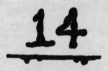

14

Mom said not to worry about losing my brain. She said we'd wait a few days before deciding what to do.

That made me feel a lot better.

That night, I was writing a homework assignment on my computer. Miss Mosely had given us a creative writing assignment. We had to write a story from someone else's point of view.

I decided to write about a typical day from Tyler's point of view. It was fun to try to get inside the mind of a dog.

A dog has an IQ of ten. That's what I learned on one of those science shows on TV. A ten IQ isn't very smart. You can't figure too many things out with an IQ of ten. That's why Tyler always looks confused and surprised.

That's why he can spend ten minutes barking at a plastic trash bag.

I leaned over my keyboard, typing away. I was

enjoying myself. I don't usually like to write papers, but this was a fun assignment.

When the phone rang, I groaned and kept typing. I waited for Mom to pick it up downstairs. But she didn't.

I stood up and walked over to the phone on my bed table. A chill froze the back of my neck.

Was it him? Was it Keith?

I remembered the first time he had called. The day I'd been hit on the head.

My hand grabbed the phone, but I didn't pick it up. I couldn't decide what to do. I didn't want to talk to him again. I wanted him to disappear.

On the sixth ring, I lifted the phone to my ear. "Hello?"

"Hi, Marco. It's me."

Another chill ran down the back of my neck. Then I recognized the voice. "Jeremy?"

"Yeah. Hi. What's up?"

"Jeremy?" I repeated.

"Yeah. You okay, Marco? I just wondered how you were doing."

"Oh. I'm okay," I told him. I sat down on the edge of my bed. "I'm feeling all right. I'm working on the creative writing assignment."

"Yeah. Me too," Jeremy replied. "Whose point of view did you choose?"

"My dog's," I replied.

He laughed. "I'm writing about my cat!"

"You think everyone in class chose an animal?" I asked. "That would be funny."

We talked and laughed about stuff for a while. Talking to Jeremy cheered me up. I was starting to feel really normal again.

"I'd better get back to work," I said after a few more minutes. I set down the phone and crossed the room to my computer.

I started to sit down — but stopped when I saw the monitor screen.

My writing — my words — had all disappeared. A face stared out at me from the screen.

Keith's face!

"No —!" I let out a cry.

And a powerful arm slid around my neck from behind. And began to tighten around my throat.

15

"Unnnnh."

I struggled to breathe.

The arm tightened around me.

I tossed up my hands. Spun around hard.

And gaped at Gwynnie.

She stepped back, grinning.

"Huh?" I choked out. "What's the big idea?"

Her grin grew wider. "Did I scare you?"

"No," I replied, still breathing hard. "I'm used to people sneaking in and strangling me from behind."

She laughed. "I wanted to surprise you. Guess I don't know my own strength."

"Sure you do," I muttered, rubbing my neck. "What are you doing here, Gwynnie?"

She dropped down heavily onto my desk chair. "Actually, I came to apologize."

"Huh?" My mouth dropped open.

"Really," she insisted. She used both hands to brush her thick black hair back over her broad shoulders. "I felt bad about my joke in class today. You know. About hitting you on the head again."

"Yes. I remember," I said, rolling my eyes.

"It was really stupid," Gwynnie continued. "I don't know why I said it. So I wanted to say I'm sorry."

"Gwynnie, you chased me after school —" I protested. "You came after me with a baseball bat and —"

"No!" she cried, jumping up from the chair. "I was running after you to apologize."

"Then why were you carrying the bat?" I demanded.

"I was up next," she explained. "That's all." Her expression changed. "Did you really think I was going to hit you on the head again?"

"Well . . ." I didn't want to tell her that was *exactly* what I thought. She'd tell everyone in school that I was afraid of her. Everyone would have a really good laugh about what a 'fraidy cat Marco is. How I ran away from someone who only wanted to apologize.

Gwynnie locked her green eyes on me. "You know, I feel bad about everything, Marco," she said softly. "I keep picturing you the other afternoon when I swung the bat and hit you. I keep picturing the way you dropped to your knees, screaming."

She sighed. "I — I was so scared. You just

lay there on the grass. You didn't move. I — I thought . . ." She glanced away.

"I'm okay," I told her. "I'm fine now. Really."

"Well, I never got a chance to say I'm sorry," Gwynnie replied. "So here I am." She raised her eyes to me. "You're really okay?"

I nodded. Then I remembered Keith.

"I have one big problem," I told Gwynnie. "This boy. He keeps following me. Calling me. Showing up in my room."

Her green eyes grew wide with surprise. "A boy? In your room?"

I nodded. "Look. His face — it's on the computer screen!" I pointed. "I was working on the writing assignment. I answered the phone. And when I came back, my writing was gone. And his face stared out at me on the screen. Look!"

Gwynnie gazed at the monitor. When she turned back to me, her expression was confused.

"Marco," she said, staring hard at me. "Your computer isn't turned on!"

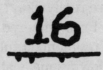

16

"No way!" I cried.

I turned to the monitor. Black. The screen was black.

No face. No words.

Gwynnie walked across the room and leaned against the window ledge. She crossed her arms in front of her. "That was a joke — right?" she demanded.

I couldn't take my eyes from the screen. Had I imagined the face? No! I *saw* it there.

I'm not crazy! I told myself.

"He did it!" I told Gwynnie, my voice shaking. "Keith. His name is Keith. He — he's playing tricks on me. He's *haunting* me!"

Gwynnie eyed me suspiciously. "Marco, when did you see him for the first time? *After* the hit on the head — right?"

"I don't care!" I cried. "He's here, Gwynnie. I saw him. He sat right there. Right on my bed. He says he lives in my basement."

56

Gwynnie shook her head. Her dark hair tumbled over her face again. "Calm down, Marco. Stop and think about it."

"I can describe him," I insisted breathlessly. "He has black hair. Same color as yours. And dark circles around his eyes. And a real serious expression."

Gwynnie *tsk-tsked*. "Just think about it," she repeated. "Why would he be here? Why would he be in your basement?"

"He told me I have to take care of him," I replied heatedly. "He said I have to take care of him for the rest of my life!"

Gwynnie narrowed her eyes at me. She didn't say anything. I could see her studying me.

And I could almost read her thoughts:

Poor Marco.

He's totally lost it.

An idea flashed into my mind.

"Gwynnie, he's down there," I said softly. "Keith is down in the basement. I know he is."

She still didn't reply.

"Come down with me?" I asked. "Please?"

She bit her bottom lip.

Gwynnie is a lot braver than I am, I told myself. She's bigger than I am. And she's meaner and stronger.

If we find Keith down in the basement, I'll feel a lot safer if Gwynnie is around.

"This is dumb," she said finally. "I should get

home. I haven't even started the creative writing assignment." She headed for the door.

"No. Wait!" I pleaded, hurrying after her. "I'm not crazy, Gwynnie. Come down to the basement with me so I can prove it."

She stopped at the doorway. "Well . . ."

"Please!" I begged again. "He's down there. We'll find him. I know we will." And then I added, "You're not afraid — are you?"

"Of course not!" Gwynnie snapped. She groaned and tossed up her hands. "Okay. Okay. Let's go down to your basement."

I *knew* that would get her.

"Come on. Hurry," Gwynnie urged. "Show me your little friend. Then I've got to get home."

I led the way to the basement stairs. Then I pulled open the door and clicked on the light.

I peered down the wooden stairway. Nothing to see down there.

But I felt a chill of fear, anyway.

"You go first," I told Gwynnie.

17

Our sneakers thudded on the wooden steps. The air grew colder as we made our way down. Mom is always complaining that we have no heat in the basement.

Gwynnie led the way, moving quickly. My hand gripping the banister, I hurried to stay close to her.

At the bottom of the stairs, I stopped short to keep from bumping into her. We both glanced around the main room.

A ceiling light had gone out. Half the room was hidden in deep shadows. I heard the *DRIP DRIP DRIP* of a faucet, coming from the laundry room at the far wall.

The sound of heavy breathing made me gasp. Then I realized the sound came from Gwynnie.

Gwynnie took a few steps into the room. Then she cupped her hands around her mouth and shouted, "Hey, boy — are you down here?"

I crept up beside her. And listened.

No reply.

"Keith?" Gwynnie shouted. "Keith? Where are you?"

I shuddered. He was down here. I knew he was. Why wasn't Gwynnie afraid?

A sudden sound made me jump. My eyes moved up to the ceiling. Gusts of wind were rattling the basement windows.

I stopped to listen to another strange sound. A mouse?

No. Just Gwynnie's sneakers squeaking over the linoleum floor.

We moved deeper into the room. I stepped up to the pool table. I peered underneath.

No one under there.

Gwynnie pulled open the pantry door beneath the stairwell. She clicked on the light and searched the shelves.

She closed the door and turned to me. "I'm starting to feel a little silly, Marco."

"He's down here," I insisted, my voice just above a whisper. "He says he lives down here. I know he's here."

Gwynnie sighed. "I'll give it a few more minutes. Then I'm out of here."

"Let's search over here," I said. "By the furnace."

We made our way across the room. The furnace stood in the dark part of the room. It rose up in front of us like some kind of gigantic creature.

60

"Keith?" Gwynnie called. "Keith — where are you hiding? Come out, come out — wherever you are!"

Her voice echoed off the dark walls. Outside, the wind howled, rattling the windows.

"Hey — wait up!" I whispered. I didn't want Gwynnie to get too far ahead of me.

She pulled open an old clothes cabinet. "Keith — are you in there?"

The smell of mothballs floated out. Gwynnie slammed the closet door shut.

"Keith? Don't be shy, Keith!" she called.

We peered behind the furnace. No one hiding back there.

"The laundry room is the only room we haven't searched," I told her.

"I'll bet he's hiding in the dryer," Gwynnie teased.

I knew she wasn't taking me seriously. But I didn't care. I was glad to have her down there with me. I never could have searched the basement on my own.

I followed her toward the laundry room against the wall. We were halfway across the floor when she stopped suddenly.

"Oh, wow!" she exclaimed. "There he is! I see him!"

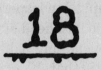

18

"Huh?" My heart leaped. I let out a gasp and spun around.

And stared at my mom's old clothing dummy.

Gwynnie laughed. "Ooops. A little mistake!"

My whole body was shaking. "You're not funny!" I managed to choke out. I tried to punch her. But she dodged away from me, laughing hard.

"Marco, give up," she said, shaking her head. "I know you're trying to scare me with this phony Keith story. But it just isn't scary enough. I know there's no one down here."

"But — but — but —" I sputtered. "You mean you didn't believe me for one second?"

"Of course not," Gwynnie replied. "Who would believe a story like that?"

"And you thought I was just trying to pay you back for hitting me on the head?" I asked shrilly.

She nodded. "You want to go to school tomorrow and tell everyone how you scared me," Gwynnie accused.

"No. You're wrong. Listen to me —" I pleaded.

"No way," she interrupted. She turned and headed toward the stairs.

"Gwynnie, listen —!" I begged, chasing after her.

She stopped at the bottom of the stairs and turned back to me. "You can't scare me, Marco," she said. Her eyes caught the light from the stairwell. A strange smile spread over her face.

"You can't scare me," she repeated. "I'll show you why."

"Excuse me?" I didn't understand. "If you'd only listen to me . . ."

"I'll show you something," Gwynnie said.

She placed both hands on the wooden banister. Then she opened her mouth. Wide.

Wider.

Her mouth stretched open. Wider . . . wider.

Until the rest of her face disappeared behind her open mouth.

Her tongue plopped heavily over her chin.

And then something pink began to pour out.

Something pink and glistening wet rolled out from the gaping mouth.

More . . . more . . . swelling as it poured out.

At first, I thought she had a big gob of bubblegum in there. But as the pink gunk flowed up from her throat, the mouth pulled open even further, and her head disappeared behind it.

And I realized . . .

I realized . . .

I realized I wasn't staring at bubblegum.

I was staring at Gwynnie's *insides*!

I saw yellow organs clinging to the glistening pink flesh. Something long and gray twisted out of her mouth, wrapped around itself.

Dark purple lungs slid over the drooping tongue.

And then her red heart — so red, so startlingly red — plopped from her open mouth, throbbing, throbbing steadily, throbbing wetly.

"Ohhhhh." I uttered a long moan of horror.

But I couldn't turn away. Couldn't take my eyes off Gwynnie as her insides poured from her mouth.

I stood there. Stood there and stared in amazement and cold horror at the pulsing, quivering organs clinging to the oozing pink flesh.

Stood there watching Gwynnie — until she had turned completely inside out.

And then I opened my mouth in an endless scream.

19

My scream rose like a shrill siren.

Gwynnie — inside out Gwynnie — quivered in front of me, quivered and pulsed.

The sound of my scream seemed to make her quiver harder, quiver like a mound of pink and yellow Jell-O.

And as I screamed, a white light flashed around us. So bright, I closed my eyes and still saw it.

Such a bright white, blinding white.

My scream cut through the whiteness. Gwynnie vanished inside it. The basement vanished too.

I sank into the white, into the shrill wail of my own cry.

And when I opened my eyes, I stared up at a white ceiling. A white ceiling light. White curtains over a half-open window, revealing gray clouds.

My throat ached. I cut off my scream.

I blinked into the new whiteness.

And Mom's face floated into view.

"Marco? Are you waking up?" she asked softly.

Her lipstick was smeared. Her eyes were blood-shot. I saw dried tear tracks on her pale cheeks.

"Waking up?" I choked out, my voice hoarse and sleep-clogged.

"You're going to be okay," Mom said, patting my chest under the blanket.

I glanced around. I was lying on my back in a bed. In a small room. A hospital room.

"You had a bad hit on the head, Marco," Mom said. "The ambulance rushed you here, to the hospital. You've been out for nearly an hour."

"Huh? I've been out?" I whispered. "You mean asleep?"

Mom nodded.

"But I was down in the basement," I protested. "Gwynnie and I were searching for the boy."

Mom's expression turned fearful. Her chin trembled. "Boy? What boy?"

"Keith," I told her. "The boy who says he lives in our basement."

"Marco, you were dreaming," Mom said.

"It — it was so frightening," I sighed.

"From your hit on the head," Mom explained. "You were out cold. It must have given you terrible nightmares."

"You mean I haven't been home?" I cried. "I haven't been in school?"

Mom eyed me carefully, studying me. "No. You've been in this hospital bed ever since you were hit."

66

She shook her head. "I warned you, Marco. I told you not to play baseball. I knew something like this would happen."

She kept on talking, but I didn't listen.

I was thinking hard. And feeling so happy.

It had all been a dream. Keith living in my basement . . . Dr. Bailey wanting to remove my brain . . .Gwynnie turning inside out . . .

All a wild, frightening dream.

It never happened. None of it.

And now it was over. And I was going to be okay.

I felt so great, I wanted to leap up from the bed. I wanted to shout and cheer and jump for joy.

But then I gazed over Mom's shoulder to the door.

And I saw . . . Gwynnie!

"Noooo!" I uttered a horrified cry.

Gwynnie was real. Gwynnie was alive! And she was coming for me, hurrying across the room to get me, an evil gleam in her eyes!

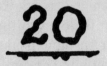

20

I let out a scream. I struggled to climb up. But the sheet and blanket were tucked in too tight.

I couldn't move.

"Mom — stop her!" I pleaded. "Please — don't let her hurt me!"

Gwynnie stepped up to the side of the bed, her eyes glowing. Mom put a hand on Gwynnie's shoulder. "Marco, what's wrong?" Mom demanded. "Why are you afraid of your own sister?"

Sister?

"No —!" I protested. "She swung the bat. She hit my head. And then —"

"I did not!" Gwynnie whined. "I wasn't the one who hit you! Are you crazy?"

Mom tugged Gwynnie back a few steps. "Gwynnie didn't do it, Marco," Mom said softly. "Gwynnie wasn't at the playground. Don't you remember?"

"That bump on his head messed up his memory," Gwynnie said. She stared hard at me, shaking her head. "Do you remember *anything*, Marco?"

"Of course," I murmured.

But I suddenly felt dizzy. As if my brain were spinning inside my head. I felt so confused. I didn't know what I remembered and what I'd forgotten.

"How much is four and four?" Gwynnie demanded.

"Gwynnie, give Marco a break," Mom scolded. She turned back to me. "You *do* remember your little sister now — right, Marco?"

Little sister?

Gwynnie was twice my size.

"Yes, I remember her," I replied. I rolled my eyes. "How could I forget her? I guess the horrible dream mixed everything up," I explained. "In my dream, she wasn't my sister. And she swung the bat that —"

"Your friend Jeremy swung the bat!" Gwynnie declared. "Don't you remember anything?"

"Jeremy?" I cried.

"It will take Marco a little while," Mom told Gwynnie. "But Dr. Bailey says he will be perfectly okay."

"But he'll be stupid," Gwynnie insisted.

Mom gasped. "Gwynnie! Why do you say that?"

Gwynnie giggled. "Because he was stupid *before* he got hit on the head!"

I let out a growl. I wanted to jump up and punch

69

Gwynnie. But the sheet was too tight. And I felt too weak.

My head throbbed. Pieces of my dream kept flashing back into my mind.

Once again, I saw Gwynnie down in the basement, turning inside out. I saw her pink and yellow insides quivering like a pile of Jell-O.

And I saw Keith, sitting on my bed. So calm and relaxed, as if the bedroom was his!

"Mom," I said, trying to force away the strange, confusing pictures. "There is no boy named Keith — is there? I mean, I don't know a boy named Keith. He doesn't live in our basement — does he?"

"Of course he does!" Gwynnie cried.

21

"Huh?" I stared at her in horror.

Gwynnie grinned. "The basement is filled with people!" she exclaimed. "Dozens of them. They call themselves The Basement Club. They stay down there until we all leave. And then they come upstairs and use our stuff."

She laughed, as if she had just made up the funniest joke.

"Stop teasing your brother," Mom scolded her. "Why are you picking on him, Gwynnie? Can't you see he's had a rough time?"

"Sorry," Gwynnie said to me, still grinning.

"She's just nervous," Mom explained. "She was very worried about you, Marco. Really."

I settled back on the pillow. "The dream . . . it seemed so real," I murmured.

"Get some rest," Mom replied tenderly. "You need time to get over this."

She waved Gwynnie to the door. "Your sister

and I will go out to the waiting room and let you get some sleep."

"But — when can I go home?" I demanded.

"Soon," Mom promised. "As soon as Dr. Bailey checks you out. He said if you're okay, you can come home right away."

"Great!" I cried.

I really wanted to get out of that hospital bed. For one thing, the tight sheets were *strangling* me. And I knew I wouldn't have such weird, disturbing dreams in my own bed.

"See you later, Marco," Gwynnie called as she stepped out the door. She instantly poked her head back in. "One last question. How much is four and four?"

"Gwynnie —!" Mom shoved Gwynnie down the hall.

"Nine!" I called after them.

Gwynnie laughed. "Hey — you got it right!"

I stared at the doorway for a long time after they left. Then I stared at the ceiling for a while, counting the white squares.

My head throbbed. But I started to feel calmer. The room stopped spinning.

I shut my eyes, and I guess I fell asleep.

The next thing I knew, I felt someone gently tapping my shoulder. I opened my eyes to find a young doctor in a white lab coat staring down at me.

"Marco? Are you awake?" he asked softly. "I'm Dr. Bailey."

He didn't look anything like the Dr. Bailey in my dream. He had wavy blond hair and bright blue eyes. He was young and tanned. He looked like an actor — a TV doctor — not a doctor in real life.

"How are you feeling?" he asked, his voice low and whispery. "A little dizzy? Do you have a headache?"

"A little," I replied.

"That's normal," he said. "Let me just check you out, Marco. Bet you're ready to go home."

"I'm ready," I declared.

"Well, let's see . . . ," Dr. Bailey said, studying my eyes. "Your eyes look nice and clear. That's a very good sign. Open your mouth, please."

I opened my mouth.

The doctor reached in with his right hand. He grabbed my tongue. And started to pull it.

"Hey —!" I tried to protest. But I couldn't speak.

His fingers tightened their grip on my tongue. And he pulled harder.

Stop! You're hurting me! What are you doing?

That's what I wanted to shout.

But all I could get out was a muffled, "Haaaaaah?"

Dr. Bailey tugged hard on my tongue. It slid out of my mouth, as long as a hot dog.

I struggled to squirm away. But he held my chest down with one hand while he pulled my tongue with the other.

Pulled . . . pulled . . .

My tongue was a yard long. It drooped down the side of the bed.

Dr. Bailey reached deeper into my mouth and pulled.

Pulled out more tongue. More . . .

Yard after yard. My tongue curled on the floor, wet and pink.

I tossed my head back and struggled to breathe.

As the doctor pulled . . . pulled more tongue from my open mouth.

More tongue. More . . .

My tongue piled up like an endless wet snake on the floor beside the bed.

Humming to himself, Dr. Bailey continued to pull.

It's a dream, I told myself. Another frightening nightmare.

I shut my eyes tight and willed myself to wake up, to lift myself from the dream.

Wake up, Marco! Wake up! Wake up!

But when I opened my eyes, the doctor still hunched beside me, pulling out my tongue. Pulling . . . pulling . . .

It wasn't a dream.

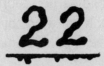

22

And then I woke up.

And stared up at the white squares on the ceiling.

I pulled myself onto my elbows. Sweat poured down my forehead. My head throbbed.

"Dr. Bailey —?" I choked out.

Gone.

Blinking away my confusion, I glanced around the room. The white curtains fluttered over the half-open window. A bed against the far wall stood empty.

All alone.

I was all alone in the hospital room.

I glanced down at the floor, expecting to see a pink coiled pile of my tongue.

No. The floor was clean. I moved my tongue against my teeth. My normal-sized tongue.

I uttered a long, relieved sigh.

I'm okay, I thought. And I'm awake. I'm finally awake.

No more disgusting nightmares.

I heard heavy footsteps in the hall. I turned to the door in time to see a *giant* enter the room!

The man smiled at me and rubbed his stubbly black beard. He had to be at least seven feet tall! He ducked his head as he stepped into the room. He had bushy black hair and thick black eyebrows that looked like caterpillars floating over his eyeglasses.

His white lab coat hung loosely over his long body. A stethoscope bobbed against his broad chest as he walked.

"Feeling a little better, Marco?" he asked. "I'm Dr. Bailey."

"Uh . . . are you the *real* Dr. Bailey?" I blurted out.

He furrowed his bushy eyebrows. "What do you mean?"

"Well . . . ," I started. "The other Dr. Bailey . . . I mean . . . the Dr. Bailey in my dream . . ."

He sat down on the edge of the bed. The mattress sank under his weight. He studied me with his eyes for a long moment. "Yes, yes. I'm a little troubled by these dreams of yours," he said finally.

He placed the end of the stethoscope on my chest and listened for a few seconds. "Heartbeat is completely normal," he reported.

He frowned. "Your mother and your sister are down in the hospital cafeteria. They'll be up in a minute. They told me about your dreams," he said quietly. "Your mom said you were a little confused by them. And frightened."

I nodded. "They were scary. And they seemed so real. The colors were so real. And . . ." I didn't know what else to say.

Dr. Bailey nodded. "I want to keep you here one more night, Marco," he said, tucking the stethoscope under his lab coat. "Your X rays are okay. I couldn't find any skull damage. The skin is bruised. But your head should heal up nicely."

"That's great!" I interrupted.

He nodded again. "Yes. But I'm a little troubled by all these strange dreams you've been having."

"So I have to stay here one more night?" I asked, disappointed.

He climbed to his feet. Standing so close to me, he appeared to be a mile high!

"Yes. One more night," he replied, scribbling some notes on a clipboard. "I'll check back with you in the morning. I'm pretty sure you will be able to leave then."

"Thank you, doctor," I said in a tiny voice. I couldn't hide how upset I felt. I really wanted to get out of that hospital.

Dr. Bailey turned at the door. "Oh. I almost forgot," he said, shaking his head.

He pulled a square envelope from the pocket of his lab coat. "This came for you, Marco. A few minutes ago. While your mom and sister were downstairs. I almost forgot to deliver it."

He handed the envelope to me. "Get some rest," he instructed. "I'll do my best to get you out of here in the morning."

I thanked him again. I watched him duck his head as he made his way out into the hall. Then I examined the envelope. It said FOR MARCO on the outside, in a handwriting I didn't recognize.

I tore the envelope open and pulled out a note. The handwriting was small and very sloppy. I squinted hard at it and read:

Dear Marco,

Please hurry home. It's time for you to start taking care of me.

I'm waiting for you in the basement.

Keith

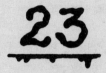

23

A few minutes later, Mom and Gwynnie walked into the room.

"We brought you a treat," Gwynnie announced. She handed me a Milky Way bar, my favorite.

"The nurse said you can eat whatever you want," Mom said. She stepped up to the bed. "Was the doctor here? What did he say?"

"He said I can probably go home in the morning," I told her. "But, Mom —?"

She narrowed her eyes at me.

"Aren't you going to eat the candy bar?" Gwynnie asked.

"Later," I replied sharply.

"But it's your favorite!" Gwynnie insisted.

I knew what she wanted. She wanted a bite!

I ignored her and gazed up at my mother. "Mom, Dr. Bailey gave me this letter. I don't understand where it came from. It's from that boy Keith. You know. The one in my dream. But that's impossible. How —?"

"What letter?" Mom interrupted. "Show it to me, Marco. Let me read it."

I reached for the letter. I had set it down on top of the blanket.

No. Not there.

I fumbled around the bed for it.

No.

I sat up and searched. Had it fallen on the floor?

No. I didn't see it there.

I lifted the pillow and peered underneath. I tugged up the sheet and blanket and searched in the bed.

"That's so weird," I murmured, shaking my head. "I had it in my hand. And I just set it down a minute ago."

Mom and Gwynnie exchanged glances.

"No. Really!" I protested.

"Maybe you should get back into bed," Mom said. "I don't think Dr. Bailey wants you walking around yet."

"But I've got to find that letter," I insisted.

"Your candy bar is melting," Gwynnie said.

"I don't care about the stupid candy bar!" I screamed. "I got a letter from that boy who says he lives in our basement. And I want to prove it to you!"

"Stop screaming, Marco," Mom scolded. "You're not thinking clearly. You need to rest."

"But — but —" I sputtered.

I turned to the door as Dr. Bailey poked his head

in. "There you are!" he smiled. "Marco, are you out of bed already? Feeling stronger, huh?"

"Dr. Bailey — tell them!" I cried. "You just brought me a letter — right? Tell them about the letter you brought me."

Dr. Bailey's heavy black eyebrows rose up to his forehead. "Letter?" he asked. "What letter?"

24

That night, I tried not to fall asleep. I didn't want any more nightmares. I didn't want to see that boy Keith again. And I didn't want to see my sister or anyone else opening their mouth and turning inside out.

I kept my eyes wide open and stared at the gray sky out the window. And listened to the sounds of the hospital outside my room.

But I fell asleep, anyway. And slept hard, without a single dream.

When I awoke the next morning, Mom and Gwynnie were already in my room. Mom was packing my bag.

I groaned and pulled myself up on one elbow.

"Wake up, Sleeping Beauty," Mom said cheerfully. "Dr. Bailey says you can go home this morning."

"Great!" I cried, my voice still hoarse from sleep. My head ached. My hand shot up to the bandage on the side of my head.

"Don't touch it," Mom warned. "Your head will hurt for a while. But you're okay."

I lowered my legs to the floor. I felt a little dizzy, but I stood up.

"Dr. Bailey says you can go back to school as soon as you feel strong enough," Mom said.

"You're so lucky!" Gwynnie exclaimed. "You missed all the tests — and a really bad-news assembly with bagpipe players."

"Get dressed," Mom instructed.

She didn't have to tell me twice. I practically dove into my clothes.

I was so happy to be going home, I wanted to sing and dance. I even hugged Gwynnie, for the first time in my life! "I'm sorry I dreamed you weren't my sister," I told her.

"Yuck! Don't hug me again," Gwynnie replied, making a face. "You're scaring me, Marco. You'd better start acting normal!"

"Don't worry," I told her. "I'll be normal. As soon as we get home, I'll be as normal as a person can be!"

And I meant it.

When we arrived home, I kissed the front door! I was so happy. I'd only been away for two days — but it seemed like two years!

Mom got to work in the kitchen, making a home-made pizza. My favorite food. Mom puts lots of cheese on her pizza, and slices of hot dogs instead of pepperoni.

She usually makes a pizza only on weekends. But today was a special day, a day to celebrate.

Jeremy came over that afternoon. He apologized for hitting me in the head with the bat.

I told him I didn't even remember how it happened.

"I'm not sure, either," Jeremy replied. "You were standing behind me. I didn't see you there at all. It was my turn at bat. I took a practice swing, and . . . *BAM*."

I struggled to remember. But it didn't come back to me.

"I'm really sorry, Marco," Jeremy apologized again.

"It wasn't your fault," I told him. "Don't blame yourself."

"Maybe you knocked some sense into him!" Gwynnie replied from the den door.

"Get out of here, Gwynnie!" I shouted. "What are you doing out there in the hall? Spying on us?"

"Why would I spy on you?" she shot back. "You're too boring!"

I think Gwynnie has a crush on Jeremy. She's always showing off when he comes over.

"Mom rented some movies. We're going to watch one now," I called to her. "Are you going to watch it with us?"

"Bor-ring!" she replied. But she plopped down on the arm of the couch, anyway. She crossed her arms in front of her chest. "What movie?"

I pulled out an Indiana Jones movie I'd seen about ten times. "This one is cool," I said. "Let's watch it again."

Mom usually doesn't let us watch movies in the middle of the afternoon. She says it's bad for our eyes.

But today was a special day.

Homemade pizza and an Indiana Jones movie. It doesn't get much better than that — right?

The three of us sat in the den, eating slice after slice and watching the movie. Mom kept interrupting every few minutes to ask how I felt.

Each time, I told her, "Fine."

But near the end of the movie, my head started to ache. I felt tired and a little shaky.

I decided I'd better take a nap. I said good-bye to Jeremy and told him I'd call him later to go over our homework. Then I went up to my room.

With a weary sigh, I sat down on the bed and pulled off my sneakers. Then I tugged down the covers.

I started to climb into bed — but I suddenly had the strange feeling I was being watched.

I turned away from the bed — and saw a boy leaning in the doorway.

"Jeremy —?" I called out.

No. As he stepped into the room, I recognized him.

Keith.

25

I blinked once.

Twice.

Trying to make him disappear.

But he crossed the room steadily, slowly, his dark eyes locked on me.

"No way!" I cried, jumping to my feet. "You can't be here! I dreamed you!"

"I know," he replied calmly.

"I dreamed you!" I shouted. "And I'm awake now. I know I'm awake!"

I pinched my arm. I scratched my cheek.

"Ow!" It hurt.

I was awake. Definitely awake. Not dreaming.

"You can't be here, Keith!" I repeated, my knees shaking, my whole body trembling. "No way you can be here. I'm awake now. And you don't exist!"

Keith stopped a few feet in front of me. "Sure, I do," he replied. A smile spread over his solemn face. His dark eyes flashed. "I live in your basement, Marco. You know that. I told you that before."

"But — but —" I sputtered. "You are not real. You were only in my dreams!"

Still smiling, Keith shook his head. "I'm real. Touch me." He held out his arm.

I hesitated. Then I reached out slowly . . . slowly . . . and squeezed his hand.

"Hey —!" I jumped back. He *was* real!

He laughed. "I told you."

"But in my dreams . . . ," I started.

"I used your dreams," Keith explained. "I communicated with you in your dreams. I put myself in your dreams."

"Wh-why?" I stammered.

His smile faded. "I wanted you to know that I was here. Waiting for you."

I didn't like the cruel expression on his face. I didn't like the way he was talking.

He frightened me.

He was *trying* to frighten me, I suddenly realized.

My heart thudded in my chest. The side of my head began to throb.

I took a step back. My legs hit the edge of my mattress. And I tumbled onto my back on the bed.

Keith quickly stepped up in front of me, blocking my way, keeping me from climbing to my feet.

"I've been waiting for you, Marco," he repeated, his eyes hard and cold. "Because you're going to take care of me. For the rest of your life."

"No —!" I shouted.

I squirmed to the side and tried to jump up.

But he was too fast for me. He moved quickly to block me.

I stared up at him in fright. "No. No way!" I repeated shrilly.

"You're going to do whatever I say, Marco," Keith insisted. He leaned over me, threatening me.

"Go away! You don't belong here! You're frightening me!" I blurted out.

"Get *used* to it!" he hissed. He leaned closer, so close his face was nearly touching mine.

"Get used to it, Marco," he said through clenched teeth. "You have no choice. I'm here. I'm real. I live in your basement. You have to take care of me now. You have to take care of everything I need."

"Nooooo!" I let out a horrified howl.

And spun out from under him.

I dropped to the floor on my knees. Then I scrambled past him and jumped to my feet.

He whirled around, and I saw the anger in his dark eyes. He uttered a fierce growl.

"Where are you going, Marco?" he demanded.

He didn't wait for an answer.

He pounced. Like an attacking animal.

I dodged away from him. Then I staggered backwards to my desk.

If only I could get to the bedroom door.

But he hunkered in the middle of the room now, panting like a wild creature, his eyes blazing.

Blocking my path.

With another low growl, he started toward me again.

I searched the room. Searched for a way to escape.

Searched for a weapon. Something to keep him away.

"You can't get away from me, Marco," he cried. "You're going to take care of me — forever!"

He dove for me again.

I leaned back against the desk. My hand tightened around a paperweight. A big, heavy stone owl that Gwynnie had given me for my last birthday.

As Keith leaped, I swung my fist with the owl paperweight.

And slammed Keith in the head with it.

His dark eyes bulged in shock.

His mouth dropped open, but no sound came out.

He slumped to the floor. Collapsed in a heap. And didn't move.

"Keith —?" I called down in a tiny, quivery voice. "Keith?"

He didn't move. His eyes stared blankly up at the ceiling.

"Keith —?"

I let the heavy stone owl drop to the floor. And then I crouched down beside the still body.

"Keith? Keith —?"

"Oh, noooo," I moaned. "What have I done?"

26

"Keith —?"

I shook his shoulders. His head bounced on the carpet. His eyes stared up at me glassily. They didn't blink.

"Nooooo!" I let out another terrified moan. And jumped to my feet.

The room spun around me. The floor tilted and bobbed. My head throbbed.

I stumbled to the door. I planned to call Mom for help.

But I turned back before I reached the doorway. And saw Keith start to change.

"Huh?" I uttered a gasp. And stared down at him in shock and horror.

His features — his eyes, his nose, his mouth — melted into the flesh of his face. Then his head slid into his neck.

Like a turtle pulling into its shell, Keith's head disappeared into his shoulders. His arms and legs slid into the trunk of his body.

His clothes fell away.

The skin on his body glimmered and turned milky, like the skin of a snail or a slug.

As I gaped in shock, the body began to wriggle across the carpet. It flopped wetly, heavily toward me.

I gasped as I saw the thick trail of yellow slime it left on the carpet behind it.

And then, before I could force my trembling legs to move, the spongy, wet creature rose up.

Stretched . . .

And wrapped itself around my waist.

"Unnnnnh." I let out a sick groan of disgust. Its sour aroma shot up to my nostrils, choking me. Its sticky wet flesh tightened around me.

I opened my mouth to scream for help.

But it choked off my air.

The odor . . . so foul and heavy. Wave after wave of it washed over me like some kind of poison gas.

I tried to kick the creature.

But my sneakers sank into the soft, gooey slime.

I punched with both fists. And tried butting it with my head.

My punches made wet *SQUISH SQUISH* sounds as my hands disappeared into the spongy body.

It was like battling a slimy, sticky sponge.

I tried wrestling it. Bending it back. Back . . .

But the foul-smelling goo stretched.

Stretched over me. Over my face.

So warm and sticky. Pulsing.
It wrapped around my head.
Covered my face. Covered my nose.
The warm, sticky slime slid up my nostrils.
I — I can't breathe! I realized.
I'm going to suffocate inside this thing!

27

I knew I didn't have much time to free myself. With a burst of strength, I swung my head back.

But the warm goo moved with me. Pressed tighter against my face. I could feel the sticky slime climbing up my nose, into my mouth.

I had to get help. But how?

I stumbled forward. Could I walk? Could I push the heaving, spongy creature with me?

If I could get downstairs . . .

My heart pounding, I forced myself forward.

Butting against the heavy blob, pushing, digging my knees into its flesh as I struggled to move.

Yes! I took a step. Then another.

Was I through the bedroom door?

I stared through the creature's milky flesh. Stared right through its thick body.

The house was a shadowy blur on the other side.

I couldn't breathe. My chest began to burn. I couldn't hold my breath much longer.

I had to keep going!

Pushing, butting it, forcing my legs to take another step ... another step ... I made my way down the hall with the creature over me.

Yes. Yes. Every step taking me closer to help. Yes ...

And then suddenly my feet lifted off the floor. I tumbled forward.

Falling! I was falling down the stairs.

The sticky creature bounced beneath me, cushioning me like a foam rubber pillow.

Down ... all the way down the stairs.

We bounced hard together at the bottom.

My head jerked free from the sticky goo.

I gasped in a mouthful of air. So cool and sweet. My lungs about to explode.

I sucked in another long breath.

And then the slime covered my face again.

I tried to roll free. But it stuck to the front of my body, wrapping itself tightly around me again.

I kicked off from the wall. Bounced forward.

Through the hall. Into the kitchen.

Mom — where are you? My desperate question.

Mom — are you home? Don't you hear me?

The creature clung to my face, to my chest. Its foul odor swept over me. A wave of dizziness made me slump to my knees.

No!

I forced myself up, carrying the weight of the spongy wet creature.

Across the kitchen. Peering through its glassy body.

Up to the kitchen counter.

And slammed it into the sharp counter edge.

I backed up — and pushed forward again. As hard as I could.

SLAM!

I drove the slimy creature into the edge of the counter.

Again. Again.

Pushing with all my strength. Then backing up and shooting forward again.

SLAM! SLAM!

Its body made a sharp squishy sound with each blow.

But it clung to me tightly, clung to my face, shutting off my air. Clung to me until I could feel my strength fade away.

One more try. One more slam into the counter.

I shot forward as hard as I could.

I heard a loud *SPLAAAT.*

And to my shock, the spongy warm goo fell off my face.

Dropped from my chest. Dropped to the floor with a heavy *PLOP.*

Gasping, sucking in air, panting so hard, my chest ached, I stared down.

And saw *two* of the milky slime creatures.

I had cut it in two.

The two halves throbbed wetly on the kitchen linoleum. They bobbed helplessly like fat insects on their backs.

"*Mom* —" I choked out. In only a whisper.

"*Mom* . . ." No sound. I couldn't force out a sound.

I reached my fingers into my throat — and pulled out a thick chunk of slimy goo. Gagging, I heaved it into the sink.

"Mom —!"

Where was she?

I heard a voice from somewhere in the house. From the den?

"Mom?"

Was she talking on the phone?

Couldn't she hear me battering the slime creature against the counter? Couldn't she hear me calling to her?

"Mom —?"

I staggered toward the door.

But I took only a step.

Before I could move farther, I felt something tighten around the legs of my jeans.

"Ohhhh!" I lowered my gaze — and saw *both* halves of the spongy slime creature wrapping around me.

I kicked out one leg. Then the other. But they clung tightly. And stretched.

Two of them now. Spreading their sticky, warm bodies up my jeans, up the front of my shirt.

I grabbed at them with both hands. And pulled.

But my hands slid off their shimmering wet flesh.

"Mom —! Gwynnie —! Somebody — help!"

They swept over my face. Two of them. Two of them now.

So heavy.

I fell to my knees. Then sank onto my back.

So heavy . . . the two of them were weighing me down.

As I thrashed and slashed at them, squirming and kicking, they melted. Melted back into one.

And spread around me. Pressing me inside.

Until I was trapped inside.

No air left . . . no air.

And then, staring helplessly through the thick slime, I saw something move across the kitchen.

Someone moving quickly. A blur of color.

Mom?

Was she in time?

Could she pull me out of this disgusting creature?

I gazed up at her from inside the thick, milky body.

Hurry, Mom.

I can't breathe.

Don't you see me here, trapped inside this goo?

Hurry.

Staring hard at the blur of color, I saw her run up to the creature. Saw her stare down, hands raised to the sides of her face.

Pull me out, Mom! I urged silently.

Pull me out — now! I pleaded.

But, no.

She just stood there.

Stood there and watched as my last bit of breath escaped my lungs.

28

"Get up, Marco," Mom ordered. She lowered her hands and pressed them against her waist.

"Get up, Marco," she repeated sternly. "What are you doing on the floor?"

"Huh?" I gasped. "Mom — help! I'm trapped inside this thing! I can't breathe!"

She stared down at me, frowning and shaking her head. "Marco, this really isn't the time for dumb games. Will you please get up off the floor?"

Games?

"Don't you see?" I cried. "Keith's head disappeared, and he turned into a big hunk of slime. I tried to get away, but he swallowed me and —"

She turned away from me and walked to the sink. I heard the water start to run.

"Mom —?"

"I'm starting to worry about you, Marco," Mom said in a low, steady voice. "You're not making any sense. Now, *get up*. I don't want you rolling on the floor like a baby!"

I sat up and gazed around.

"Hey —!" I let out a startled cry.

No slime creature.

I rubbed the floor with both hands. The floor was perfectly dry.

I'm having another dream, I told myself.

The glob of slime wasn't real. Our wrestling match down the stairs didn't happen. The whole thing was another disgusting dream.

I'm not sitting on the floor in the kitchen. I'm asleep in my bed, dreaming this.

And now I'm going to wake up and end it.

Wake up!

Wake up, Marco! I ordered myself.

I climbed to my feet. Mom was at the sink, drinking a tall glass of water.

Wake up, Marco!

If this was a dream, why couldn't I escape from it?

I turned — and slammed my forehead into a cabinet.

"Owww!" The pain exploded in my head, shot down my neck, my back.

"I'm *not* dreaming," I murmured out loud.

Mom turned from the sink. "What did you say?"

"I'm not dreaming," I repeated, feeling dazed.

"At least you are standing up," Mom replied. She studied me. "Does your head hurt, Marco?"

Yes. It hurt because I slammed it into a cabinet. But I said, "No. I'm fine, Mom."

And then I ran out of the kitchen. I had to get out of there. I had to think. I had to be alone and figure this out.

"Marco —?" Mom called after me.

But I didn't turn back. I ran up the stairs and into my room. And I slammed the bedroom door behind me.

"Marco, take it easy," a voice said.

I gasped and raised my eyes to the bed. Keith sat cross-legged on the blanket, the pillow between his hands.

"Sit down," he said, motioning to my desk chair. "Take a deep breath. Relax. We're going to spend a long time together. The rest of your life."

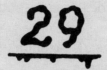

29

"Am I dreaming?" I asked in a tiny voice.

Keith didn't reply. He pointed to the chair. "Sit down," he ordered.

I glanced at the door. I thought about escaping.

But I suddenly felt so tired, so totally weak and weary.

My legs started to give way. My whole body trembled.

"I'm sooooo tired," I moaned. I turned back to Keith. "You win," I murmured. "You've beaten me."

He smiled and pointed again to the chair.

I slumped into it with a long sigh. "I can't fight you," I told him wearily. "I don't know if I'm dreaming or awake. And I don't have the strength to find out."

His smile grew wider. A victory smile, I guess. His dark eyes flashed.

"You win," I repeated sadly. "I'll do whatever you want."

He jumped to his feet and crossed the room. Then he patted me on the shoulder, as if I were his puppy dog. "Smart boy," he said.

He stood in front of me and crossed his arms. His grin was frozen on his face. "I knew you'd see it my way," he said. "Because you are a very smart boy, Marco."

I lowered my head. I couldn't stand seeing that sick grin on his face.

"I know you will take very good care of me," Keith continued. "I know you will do whatever I tell you to. For as long as you live."

He suddenly spun away and started to the door.

"Where are you going?" I demanded weakly.

"I'm going down to the basement," he replied. "Where I live. And do you know what I'm going to do?"

"No," I choked out.

"Guess," he demanded.

"I can't guess," I snapped. "Give me a break."

"I'm going down to the basement and make a list of all the things you can do for me right away," Keith said. "You wait here, Marco. When I finish my list, I will come back and we can go over it together."

"Right," I muttered under my breath. I rolled my eyes.

Was he serious about this? Did he really expect me to be his slave — forever?

He stopped at the door and turned back to me.

"Before I go, there's just one thing I want to show you," he said.

He took a few steps back into the room. Then he opened his mouth wide.

Shiny pink stuff poured out of his mouth. For a second, I thought he was blowing a bubblegum bubble.

But I quickly realized what was happening.

His glistening, wet insides poured out of his mouth. Yellow organs clung to the pink flesh. His purple heart plopped out from between his teeth, pulsing inside a thick web of blue ropelike veins.

I stared in horror, watching him turn inside out.

Then I started to scream.

And Keith opened his mouth — teeth on the outside — and he screamed too.

30

I opened my eyes and blinked. My eyes were dry and caked. My mouth felt as dry as cotton.

I must have been sleeping a long time, I told myself.

Still lying flat, I stretched my arms out. The muscles ached.

My head ached.

With a groan, I lifted my head off the pillow. Then I raised myself up onto both elbows.

"Whoa . . . ," I murmured. The basement slowly came into focus. I felt so dizzy . . . dizzy and weak.

"Keith — you're awake!"

I heard Mom's voice. And then she popped into view.

I opened my mouth to greet her, but only coughed. I cleared my throat.

"You're finally awake, Keith," Mom said. "I've been waiting for so long."

I shook my head hard, trying to shake away my

confusion. I glanced around, struggling to focus my eyes.

Yes. Here I was. Safe and sound in the basement, where Mom and I live.

But what had happened to me? Why had I been asleep for so long?

Strange pictures floated through my mind.

"Mom —" I choked out. "Mom, I had such terrible nightmares."

She tenderly brushed my hair off my forehead. Her hand felt warm and smooth. "What did you dream?" she asked softly.

"I — I dreamed that Marco was hit in the head with a baseball bat," I stammered.

Mom bit her bottom lip. "You dreamed about Marco?" she asked, staring hard at me.

I nodded. "Yes. Marco was hit by a bat, and I —"

"But *you* were hit by a bat, Keith," Mom interrupted. "Not Marco."

"Everything was turned around in the dream," I told Mom. "I dreamed that I went up to Marco's room. And I told him who I was. I told him I live in his basement."

Mom sat down on the edge of my cot. "Then what happened?" she asked.

"He started fighting me," I told her. "Marco was horrible to me. He started wrestling me. And he pulled me down the stairs. I was so *frightened*!"

Mom narrowed her eyes at me sternly. "Keith, I

warned you — didn't I? I warned you never to play with humans."

"Yes, but —" I started.

She raised a hand to silence me.

"Never play with humans, Keith," Mom scolded. "You're a monster. You should never forget it." She sighed. "Just because you look exactly like a human doesn't mean you can be friends with the humans."

"I know. I know," I grumbled.

How many times had I heard this boring lecture before? At least a hundred!

"I warned you never to play ball with Marco and the other humans," Mom continued. "But you didn't listen to me. And look — look what happened."

I raised my hand and felt the bandage on the side of my head.

"You were hit in the head with a bat, Keith," Mom said, her voice trembling. "You were badly hurt. It's no wonder you had terrible nightmares."

"Mom, please —" I tried to sit up.

But she gently forced me back onto my back. "You can't go up and play with the humans," she continued her lecture. Once Mom starts, it's impossible to stop her. "We have to be so careful, Keith. So careful."

"I know! I know!" I cried. "I know the whole lecture, Mom. We're monsters, and we live in Marco and Gwynnie's basement. And if they ever find out we're down here, they'll get frightened and chase us away."

Mom frowned at me. "I know it's tempting to go up there and play with them," she said. "But I hope you've learned your lesson. You had me so worried this time, Keith."

"I'm sorry, Mom. I'll be careful from now on," I promised.

That seemed to make her happy. She smiled at me.

"Okay," she said. "You need your rest. Turn inside out and get some sleep."

"Okay," I agreed.

I said good-night to her and watched her disappear to the other side of the basement.

Then I opened my mouth and began to turn inside out. It felt so good to let my insides pour out. So clean and refreshing.

My heart and arteries slid from between my teeth. My stomach was halfway out my mouth — when I heard a sound.

No!

A sound on the basement stairs!

I glanced up — and saw Marco standing there.

Did he see me?

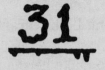

31

Staring hard at the figure on the basement stairs, I quickly sucked up my insides. My heart and veins slid back into my body. Then I swallowed my lungs.

Did Marco see me?

Yes.

His eyes bulged with shock. His mouth hung open.

A wave of panic swept over me. A chill ran down my back.

This is our worst nightmare, I thought. I've been caught. I've been seen by a human.

Now what?

I stared back at Marco and waited for him to speak.

It took him a long time. He gripped the banister and held on to it tightly. He squinted across the gray basement at me, squinted hard as if he didn't believe what he was seeing.

"Who are you?" he asked finally in a small, frightened voice.

I swallowed hard.

What should I say? How should I answer?

I had to think fast.

"Who are you?" he repeated, a little louder, a little stronger.

"Uh . . . you're dreaming!" I called to him.

He squinted harder at me.

"Go back upstairs," I told him. "It's just a dream."

Would he believe me?

About R.L. Stine

R.L. Stine is the most popular author in America. He is the creator of the *Goosebumps*, *Give Yourself Goosebumps*, *Fear Street*, and *Ghosts of Fear Street* series, among other popular books. He has written more than 100 scary novels for kids. Bob lives in New York City with his wife, Jane, teenage son, Matt, and dog, Nadine.

Add *more*

to your collection . . .
A chilling preview of
what's next from
R.L. STINE

MONSTER BLOOD IV

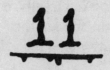

11

Evan stared at the window, stared at Andy outside in the darkness. Tapping on the glass. Tapping so urgently.

Evan jumped from the small foldout bed. His legs were tangled in the blanket. He stumbled and had to grab the edge of Kermit's dresser to catch his balance.

One foot had fallen asleep. He dragged it, limping to the window. He silently pushed open the window, careful not to wake Kermit.

Kermit snored away, *glugging* and whistling. He had kicked his blanket to the floor. He had fallen asleep with his glasses on.

Evan leaned out into the darkness. A gust of cold wind made him shiver.

"Andy — what are you doing here?" he cried out."

"Get dressed," Andy ordered. "Hurry, Evan. I have to show you something."

"Huh?" He glanced back at Kermit's clock radio. "It's almost midnight!"

Andy raised a finger to her lips. "Sssshhhh. Hurry. Get dressed. I think you'll want to see this."

She held up a can. A blue plastic can.

Evan groaned. "You really came here in the middle of the night for another joke? Give me a break, Andy. What's going to spring out at me *this* time?"

But then he saw the serious expression on Andy's face.

"It isn't a joke — is it?" he whispered.

She shook her head.

"It's Monster Blood — right?" Evan demanded.

Andy nodded. "I think so. The can — it looks the same."

Evan spun away from the window. He pulled on jeans and a sweatshirt right over his pajamas. His hands trembled as he tied his shoes.

He grabbed his down jacket from the closet. And climbed out the window.

"I was dreaming about Monster Blood," he told Andy.

She bit her bottom lip. "This isn't a dream," she replied quietly.

Evan shivered. It was a cold, clear night.

Andy wore her magenta windbreaker and a pair of silvery leggings. She had a red wool ski cap pulled down over her short brown hair.

She raised the plastic can to Evan. "I think it's the real thing. I hurried over as soon as I was sure my parents were asleep."

"Where did you get it?" he whispered.

"Behind the lab on Peachtree where my dad works. We were picking him up before dinner. I was waiting in the parking lot behind the lab. I found this in a whole pile of stuff."

"You didn't open it — did you?" Evan demanded.

"No way," she replied. She tried to hand him the can. But he waved it away.

"I don't want it," Evan told her. "Why did you bring it over here?"

Andy shrugged. "I thought after this afternoon, you might want to pay Conan back for being such a big jerk."

"Yes, I do want to pay Conan back," Evan admitted.

"So use the Monster Blood," Andy urged. "You can put a little of it in his lunch at school. You can —"

"No way!" Evan cried. "Conan is already a *mountain*! I don't want to make him any BIG-GER!"

The light faded from Andy's dark eyes. "I guess you're right. But we could put Monster Blood in his bed. Or —"

"Stop!" Evan ordered. "It's too dangerous. I don't want to use Monster Blood on Conan. Kermit and I have another plan for Conan. A really good plan."

"What is it?" Andy demanded eagerly.

"I'll tell you as soon as you get rid of the Monster Blood," Evan told her. "I really don't want that stuff around. Go hide it someplace where no one will ever find it."

"But, Evan —" Andy protested.

Evan didn't let her finish. "You know what will happen if that can gets opened," he said firmly. "It will bubble up. And it will grow and grow, and we won't be able to stop it."

"Okay, okay." Andy rolled her eyes. "I'll take it home. I'll find a good hiding place."

"Promise?" Evan demanded, eyeing her sharply.

"Promise," she repeated, raising her right hand.

"Hey — what's that?" a voice called from behind them.

Evan spun around and saw Kermit scramble out the open window.

Kermit grabbed the blue can from Andy's hand.

"Cool!" he cried. "Monster Blood! Is it real?"

He didn't wait for an answer.

He gripped the can tightly — and pulled off the lid.

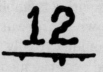

12

"No! Don't do that!" Evan screamed.

Too late.

"Close it up!" Evan cried frantically. "Close the can — quick!"

Kermit stood staring into the open can. "It's too dark. I can't see anything."

"Give me that!" Evan ordered. He leaped forward and tried to swipe the can away.

He grabbed the can — but knocked the lid from Kermit's hand.

Kermit made a wild grab for the lid. But a gust of wind blew it out of his reach.

As Evan gaped in horror, the wind lifted the plastic lid . . . lifted it over their heads.

"Noooooo!" He let out a long wail as the lid spun crazily above them. He made a wild grab. Another. Missed.

The wind carried the lid up to the slanted roof of the house. It hit the shingles. Slid down a few feet. And came to a rest in the metal rain gutter.

"I don't believe this," Evan muttered.

"I'll get the ladder from the garage," Kermit offered. He took off across the dew-wet grass.

"Hurry!" Evan cried.

"The Monster Blood — it's moving!" Andy exclaimed, pointing with a trembling finger.

Evan gazed down at the can gripped tightly in his hand. He couldn't really see inside. Dark clouds had drifted over the moon, blocking out the light.

Evan brought the can close to his face. And gasped.

"Andy — it's *blue*!"

"Huh?" She pressed close to him. Their heads banged as they both eagerly stared into the can.

Yes. The thick glop inside the can was blue — not green.

It made a sick *plopping* sound as it rolled from side to side, like an ocean wave.

"It — it's trying to get out!" Andy stammered.

"Hurry, Kermit!" Evan called.

Kermit came running from the garage, an aluminum ladder tilted over one shoulder.

"Why is it blue?" Andy asked.

The thick goo lapped at the side of the can. As Evan stared in horror, it splashed up over the top.

"Kermit — please hurry! Get the lid!" he cried.

Kermit propped the ladder against the side of the house. Then he turned back to them. "Someone else has to climb up," he called.

"Just *do* it!" Evan screamed frantically. "The stuff is spilling out over the top!"

"But I'm afraid of heights!" Kermit declared.

Evan rolled his eyes. "It isn't that high. Just climb up, and —"

"I can't!" Kermit whined. "Really!"

"I'll do it." Andy ran to the ladder. Kermit held it steady for her.

Evan watched her scramble up. The Monster Blood bobbed and plopped in the can. The clouds rolled away from the moon. It was definitely bright blue, Evan saw.

And definitely trying to raise itself out of the can.

Andy climbed up to the gutter. Holding the ladder with her right hand, she reached out to the lid with her free hand.

Reached . . . reached . . .

And the wind blew the lid from the gutter.

"Noooo —!" Andy screamed. She grabbed for it. Lost her balance.

Grabbed the sides of the ladder with both hands.

The lid spun crazily in the air. Then it swooped down to the grass.

"I've got it!" Kermit cried. He dove for it and grabbed it in one hand.

"Yes!" Evan cried happily. "Put it on the can — quick!"

Andy carefully lowered herself rung by rung.

She reached the ground, turned, breathing hard, and hurried back to Evan.

Kermit came running over with the lid.

But before he reached Evan, a voice rang out from the yard across from his.

"Hey — what's going on?"

Evan looked up to see Conan running across the grass.

"Oh, no!" Evan moaned, and the Monster Blood can fell out of his hand.

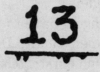

13

With a gasp, Evan bent to pick up the can.

Had the blue Monster Blood spilled out?

No.

He lifted it carefully, holding one hand over the open top.

Conan stopped at the edge of the yard. "What are you three babies doing out so late?" he demanded. "I'll tell your mommies!"

"Give us a break, Conan," Andy called. "We're not bothering you!"

"Your *face* is bothering me!" Conan shot back. Then his eyes fell on the can in Evan's hand. "What's that?"

Evan nearly dropped the can again. "This? Uh . . . nothing. . . . It's . . ."

Evan's mind went blank. He couldn't think of a good lie to tell Conan.

Kermit grabbed the can away from Evan. "It's candy," he told Conan. "Blue Fruit Roll in a Barrel! We saw it on TV, and it's awesome."

"Give me some!" Conan ordered. He reached out his big hand.

"No way!" Kermit teased him, pulling the can back. "We're not sharing with you!"

He pretended to lick the blue candy. "Wow. That's really excellent!"

"Guess I'm going to have to take it from you," Conan declared menacingly. He took a step toward them, his hand outstretched. "Give it."

"Are you crazy?" Evan whispered to Kermit. "Why did you tease him? Now he's going to take it and —"

"No problem," Kermit whispered back. A sly grin spread over his face. "Watch."

"Give it," Conan thundered, waving his outstretched hand. He took another step toward them. Another.

Evan heard the crackle of electricity before he saw the white spark.

Conan's eyes bulged. His hands shot up. His knees buckled.

"Urg. Urg." He uttered two strange cries as Kermit's invisible electric fence zapped him again.

Conan staggered back, gasping for breath. His broad chest heaved up and down. He reminded Evan of a bull about to charge.

Kermit raised the can and pretended to eat the Monster Blood again. "Wow. That is *excellent*!" he declared.

Conan glared at the three of them. Even across

the dark yard, Evan could see the fury on his face.

But the bull couldn't charge. Couldn't get to them. Not as long as the electric fence was turned on.

Conan balled his hands into fists. "You're history," he called to them. "All three of you. You're roadkill."

He spun around. Swinging his fists hard at his sides, he stomped into his house.

Andy let out a sigh of relief. "That was pretty good!" she told Kermit.

A high, shrill giggle escaped Kermit's throat. "Yeah. Not bad!"

"There's just one problem," Evan murmured. "We're roadkill if we ever leave this backyard!"

He turned to Kermit. "Give me back the can. We'd better close it —"

Evan gasped.

The can in Kermit's hand! He was holding it upside down!

Evan grabbed for it.

Too late.

With a sick *PLOP*, the blue gunk dropped out of the can.

It landed on the grass in front of Evan's feet. He stared down at it as it quivered. Quivered and shook, like blue Jell-O.

It glowed in the light from the moon. Glowed bright blue.

Bobbed and trembled.

And grew.

"It's . . . changing shape!" Andy cried. She leaned forward, resting her hands on her knees, and gazed down wide-eyed at it.

The blue blob wiggled. It rolled over once, moving away from Evan.

And grew some more.

It rolled again. Wiggled from side to side.

And then rose up. Up . . . as if trying to stand.

"I don't *believe* this!" Evan choked out. "It's some kind of *creature*!"

"You're right!" Kermit agreed. "It's ALIVE!"

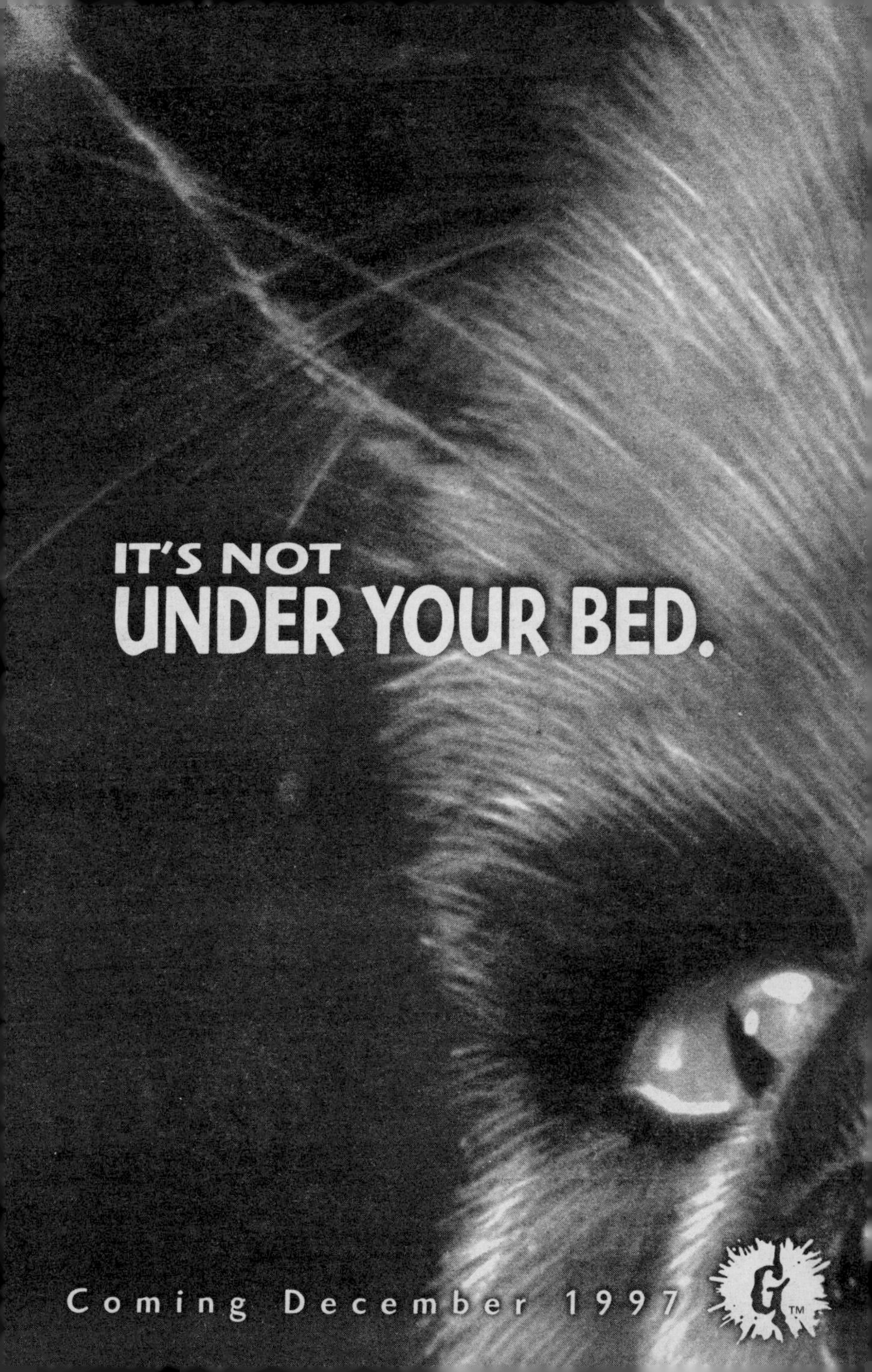
IT'S NOT
UNDER YOUR BED.
Coming December 1997
G™

Don't let any Goosebumps® books CREEP past you!

$3.99 EACH

Scare me, thrill me, mail me GOOSEBUMPS now!

Available wherever you buy books, or use this order form.
Scholastic Inc., P.O. Box 7502, Jefferson City, MO 65102

Please send me the books I have checked above. I am enclosing $_____ (please add $2.00 to cover shipping and handling). Send check or money order—no cash or C.O.D.s please.

Name _____ Age _____

Address _____

City _____ State/Zip _____

Please allow four to six weeks for delivery. Offer good in the U.S. only. Sorry, mail orders are not available to residents of Canada. Prices subject to change.

GIVE YOURSELF
Goosebumps®

...WITH 20 DIFFERENT SCARY ENDINGS IN EACH BOOK!

R.L. STINE

☐ BCD55323-2	#1	*Escape from the Carnival of Horrors*	
☐ BCD56645-8	#2	*Tick Tock, You're Dead!*	
☐ BCD56646-6	#3	*Trapped in Bat Wing Hall*	
☐ BCD67318-1	#4	*The Deadly Experiments of Dr. Eeek*	
☐ BCD67319-X	#5	*Night in Werewolf Woods*	
☐ BCD67320-3	#6	*Beware of the Purple Peanut Butter*	
☐ BCD67321-1	#7	*Under the Magician's Spell*	
☐ BCD84765-1	#8	*The Curse of the Creeping Coffin*	
☐ BCD84766-X	#9	*The Knight in Screaming Armor*	
☐ BCD84768-6	#10	*Diary of a Mad Mummy*	
☐ BCD84767-8	#11	*Deep in the Jungle of Doom*	
☐ BCD84772-4	#12	*Welcome to the Wicked Wax Museum*	
☐ BCD84773-2	#13	*Scream of the Evil Genie*	
☐ BCD84774-0	#14	*The Creepy Creations of Professor Shock*	
☐ BCD93477-5	#15	*Please Don't Feed the Vampire!*	
☐ BCD84775-9	#16	*Secret Agent Grandma*	
☐ BCD93483-X	#17	*Little Comic Shop of Horrors*	
☐ BCD93485-6	#18	*Attack of the Beastly Baby-sitter*	
☐ BCD93489-9	#19	*Escape from Camp Run-for-Your-Life*	
☐ BCD93492-9	#20	*Toy Terror: Batteries Included*	
☐ BCD93500-3	#21	*The Twisted Tale of Tiki Island*	
☐ BCD21062-9	#22	*Return to the Carnival of Horrors*	
☐ BCD39774-5	#23	*Zapped in Space*	
☐ BCD39775-3	#24	*Lost in Stinkeye Swamp*	

$3.99 EACH

Scare me, thrill me, mail me GOOSEBUMPS now!

Available wherever you buy books, or use this order form.

Scholastic Inc., P.O. Box 7502, Jefferson City, MO 65102

Please send me the books I have checked above. I am enclosing $_____ (please add $2.00 to cover shipping and handling). Send check or money order—no cash or C.O.D.s please.

Name _____Age_____

Address _____

City _____State/Zip _____

Please allow four to six weeks for delivery. Offer good in the U.S. only. Sorry, mail orders are not available to residents of Canada. Prices subject to change.

GYGB597

Log on for Scares!
Scholastic presents
Goosebumps
ON THE WEB!
http://www.scholastic.com/Goosebumps
The latest books!
Start your own Goosebumps reading club!
Author R.L. Stine's tips on writing!
Really gross recipes!
Craft ideas!
How to get Goosebumps stuff: sportswear, CD-ROMs, video releases and more!
Exclusive contests!
Interactive word games and activities!
GWEB1296

Reader Beware—

THREE NEW CHILLING SCARES COMING YOUR WAY THIS DECEMBER!

Goosebumps®

R.L. Stine

Goosebumps #62: Monster Blood IV

More Monster Blood thrills! The blood is back and this time it's blue! A shiny wet giant slug is growing bigger and bigger until...POP! Now there are two and they're multiplying by the minute!

Give Yourself Goosebumps #24: Lost in Stinkeye Swamp

Your new swamp-side house is hiding a few secrets—hidden treasure *and* an evil curse! Should you open the 200-year-old diary or look in the magic telescope? More than 20 different endings featuring swamp creatures, scorpions, and a ghost!

Goosebumps Presents TV Book #17: Calling All Creeps!

Why did Ricky try to play that joke on Tasha? Now the joke's on him—the Creeps are crank-calling him. And these creeps are more than creepy—they're icky lizards!

Look for these books in bookstores everywhere (or else!).

SCHOLASTIC

 PARACHUTE